W9-CYC-305

Keri,
You are the light!
Love,
Deb

The End of the Beginning

DEBORAH O'BRIEN

BALBOA.PRESS
A DIVISION OF HAY HOUSE

Copyright © 2021 Deborah O'Brien.

All rights reserved. No part of this book may be used or reproduced by any means, graphic, electronic, or mechanical, including photocopying, recording, taping or by any information storage retrieval system without the written permission of the author except in the case of brief quotations embodied in critical articles and reviews.

Balboa Press books may be ordered through booksellers or by contacting:

Balboa Press
A Division of Hay House
1663 Liberty Drive
Bloomington, IN 47403
www.balboapress.com
844-682-1282

Because of the dynamic nature of the Internet, any web addresses or links contained in this book may have changed since publication and may no longer be valid. The views expressed in this work are solely those of the author and do not necessarily reflect the views of the publisher, and the publisher hereby disclaims any responsibility for them.

The author of this book does not dispense medical advice or prescribe the use of any technique as a form of treatment for physical, emotional, or medical problems without the advice of a physician, either directly or indirectly. The intent of the author is only to offer information of a general nature to help you in your quest for emotional and spiritual well-being. In the event you use any of the information in this book for yourself, which is your constitutional right, the author and the publisher assume no responsibility for your actions.

Any people depicted in stock imagery provided by Getty Images are models, and such images are being used for illustrative purposes only. Certain stock imagery © Getty Images.

Scriptures taken from New Revised Standard Version

Print information available on the last page.

ISBN: 978-1-9822-6656-1 (sc)
ISBN: 978-1-9822-6654-7 (hc)
ISBN: 978-1-9822-6655-4 (e)

Library of Congress Control Number: 2021913336

Balboa Press rev. date: 07/08/2021

To my readers and the beautiful souls in all of you.

CONTENTS

PREFACE

hen the pandemic hit, I knew I wanted to write a book to help people navigate all the fear and uncertainty we suddenly faced. I went to Staples, bought twenty yellow notebooks and several black pens, then prayed for inspiration and began writing. What emerged from my heart was a fictional story about two people whose chance meeting and subsequent relationship illustrates the virtues I find have helped me cope during this uncertain time.

My first book was a memoir entitled *Bliss: Behind the Mask*. I was tempted to call this book *Fear: Behind the Mask* because many people I have met during this time have fear in their eyes behind their mask. Even watching the news had become upsetting, as newscasters began speaking with a scary tone in their voices, spreading more fear than actual information. After a while, I stopped watching the news; but I knew I couldn't continue turning a blind eye to what was happening in our world.

What bothered me most was how people were becoming numb and accepting uncivilized behavior as normal. Strength of character and virtue are now old fashioned. How did that happen? I don't know, but I do know that by practicing these old-fashioned but powerful virtues, our world can become civilized again, and that's what my story focuses on.

At the end of each chapter, you will find reflections that ask you to look within and life- changing action tips that will strengthen your coping skills and your character. It is my hope that when you practice these virtues you will witness a profound change in your life and in our world. We're all in this together.

ACKNOWLEDGMENT

This book would not be possible without the help of my dear daughter-in-law, Susan O'Brien, who spent long hours typing my handwritten manuscript. If I had to type it, it probably wouldn't be published for at least another year. I am kind of like a dinosaur. I don't like using computers. They make my palms get all sweaty.

Thank you, Susan. I appreciate all your help, from reading my early drafts to typing, editing, critiquing, and proofreading. I am grateful for all your love, support, patience, and generosity of spirit, but most of all, I am grateful for you in my life.

CHAPTER 1

Nonjudgmental

The vindictive voice inside her head screamed, *You loser! Look how you wrecked your life!* Joanne slumped in the kitchen chair and clutched her queasy stomach with a trembling hand. Thinking about the questions she might be asked and how she would answer them truthfully under oath made her lose her appetite. *I'd give anything for a cigarette right now.*

After she took a few deep breaths, she placed her elbow on the table. Resting her chin on her hand, she stared at the stale bran muffin. Like her heart, it had hardened. With a fork, she poked a raisin, but when she popped it into her dry mouth, she struggled to swallow it. Joanne pushed the plate away and thought, *Oh, well. Maybe it's not a good idea to eat bran today anyway.*

Ignoring the knots in her stomach, she grabbed the keys and bolted out of her apartment. The heavy door slipped from her sweaty palm and slammed behind her with a loud bang, sending a jolt through her body right down to her toes. Even the hallway reverberated with the deafening sound, but soon all Joanne heard was her lawyer's dire warning like a broken record. "Don't be late!"

As she dashed to her car, her nosey neighbor Louise waved her down.

"Hey, what's the big rush?" Louise yelled from across the parking lot.

Yikes! What if that blabbermouth discovers my secret? She gave her a dismissive stare. With her hands on her hips, she twirled around and asked, "Do these pants make my butt look big?"

"No, you look very professional today. Got an important client?"

"Yeah," she lied as she unlocked the car.

When she got into her convertible, she pressed the button to lower the top but kept the windows up to prevent her hair from getting blown around as she drove. She was backing out of her apartment parking spot when she heard her neighbor shout, "Do you hear them singing?"

"Who?"

"The cicadas!"

"Oh yeah." Joanne knew the rasping, buzzing sound emanating from the trees was a sure sign the day promised to be hot as hell.

Upon arriving at the federal building, she stopped her car to read the sign on the front door. The print was so small she couldn't read it. Searching through her purse, she found her glasses but still couldn't make out what the sign said. In a huff, she got out of the car, slammed the door, and marched up the front steps. The sign said the building wasn't open to the public until nine o'clock. With all her strength, she pulled and pulled on the door, but it wouldn't budge. She was locked out. Just then, a sharp twinge shot through her chest.

Getting back into her car, she turned on the air conditioner and sat with her eyes closed but was startled by a loud rap on the car window. Her eyes popped open to see a police officer crouched down beside the driver's side door of her Mercedes.

"Lady, you can't park here. The parking lot is down there," he said, motioning to his left.

"I know. I was just leaving."

As she drove off, she adjusted her Chanel sunglasses with her middle finger and threw the policeman a dirty look over her shoulder. Her smug sense of satisfaction didn't last long as a gnawing sensation grew in her stomach. She told herself she was just hungry, but deep down, she knew it was remorse taking hold. And just like that, she felt like crap. Joanne wondered why she had reacted so rudely when she knew that the officer was only doing his duty.

Driving into the parking lot, she found it was already full, and she was at a loss for what to do. As her desperation grew, her chubby fingers clutched the steering wheel, and she shook it with all her might. "God, please help me!" she screeched through clenched teeth.

She took a few deep breaths, put the top up on the convertible, and drove around the crime-ridden neighborhood to look for a parking spot. It took her several minutes until she found an available meter. She turned off her car but realized that she didn't dare get out. She sat with her seat belt on, staring straight ahead at the boarded-up windows of an old tenement house. *At least I am here now.*

She freshened up with a quick spritz of her favorite watermelon facial mist and a few sips of lemonade from her glass water bottle. Fumbling in her bag for her powder compact, she grumbled, "I can't find a dang thing in this friggin' mess." She dumped the contents of her bag onto the passenger seat and tossed items to the floor until she found it. But when she popped it open and examined herself in the tiny mirror, she could only say, "Omigosh!" The humidity had turned her champagne-blond curls into little golden ringlets, giving her the look of Goldilocks. With her button nose and big dimples, she was a cute as could be!

As she reapplied her signature hot-pink lipstick, she caught a glimpse of something out of the corner of her eye. Outside her car, what appeared to be a decrepit old man staggered by. *There but for the grace of God go I*, she thought, and then she said a brief prayer for him in a sudden and unexpected surge of compassion. She watched as he moved on down the sidewalk.

Joanne lowered the window to breathe in some fresh air but was met with a horrible, stale stench. *If sin had a scent, this would be it!* It occurred to her that the awful odor was the smell of the coastal city in decay. New Bedford, Massachusetts was spiraling out of control. She could relate to that image. *Just like my life spinning out of control in my topsy-turvy world.* A single tear trickled down her cheek. From the depths of her soul, she cried out to God, "I am so sorry! Please—"

The sound of a text arriving on her phone interrupted her pleading prayer. It was from her attorney saying he would be delayed. She sighed as she responded with a thumbs-up emoji. *He probably stopped off somewhere for a donut and coffee.* Her attorney was a roly-poly little man with an appetite as big as his ego. She wished she had the confidence in him that he so clearly had in himself.

One glance at her watch and she knew it was time to face the music. *I'd better not be late.* She locked her car and began walking up the hill to the federal building, humming softly to calm herself. Pondering the irony of possibly getting mugged as she walked to her bankruptcy hearing, she looked up from her thoughts and noticed a crowd of people milling around the front of the building. By eight thirty, a long queue had formed, wrapping around the corner of the building like a snake around a branch. Normally, Joanne was talkative and friendly in a crowd, but today she was determined not to make eye contact or start a conversation with anyone. Just as well, as no one looked particularly friendly. Standing at the end of the line, she swayed a little, shifting her weight from one foot to the other as she stared at the ground.

A short, scrappy guy with a goatee and mischievous twinkle in his eye got in line behind her and said jokingly, "Lady, settle down! You're making the rest of us more nervous than we already are!" In a boisterous voice, he added, "You got ants in your pants or somethin'?"

His remark stimulated a ripple of chuckling in the crowd.

Joanne gave him a fake smile and hoped that she looked like it didn't bother her.

When the line finally showed signs of moving forward, she could barely take a step without stumbling since they had become squished together like sardines in a tin can. Behind her, the jokester was so close she felt his breath on her neck. *What the heck?* He reeked of booze, and it oozed out through his pores. *I bet he's some low-level drug dealer.* She tried to inch forward to create some space between the two of them. In contrast, the woman in front of her was stunning, and Joanne began to compare herself to her. She noticed the gentle upsweep of the woman's pin-straight hair into a casual French twist, and without any warning, a pang of envy assaulted Joanne. *She is making me sick. She probably went bankrupt paying for all her plastic surgery.*

Easily six feet tall, the willowy platinum-blond appeared cool and comfortable in a white, gauzy sundress while others around her were sweating from the heat or nerves or both. *I guess her lawyer didn't advise her about what's appropriate to wear to court.* Joanne's lawyer had recommended that she wear something subdued and neutral, preferably a suit. Since she didn't own anything like that, she went to her local thrift shop and picked up a well-worn, practical-looking suit. Unfortunately, while the suit gave the impression of a conservative woman, worsted wool was not the fabric of choice during the heat wave. Now tiny beads of sweat were making mini pools in the cups of her padded bra. Beige was not her color, but one has few choices at a thrift shop. It drained any life out of her face and made her look frumpy.

Humph. I wouldn't look so bad if I didn't have to stand next to this skinny Gwyneth Paltrow wannabe.

Over the years, Joanne had put in a great deal of effort, energy, time, and money to find her true identity. Every day she was bombarded with tempting emails promising to help her, and all she had to do was "click here." She never hesitated before signing up for one irresistible offer after irresistible offer. Coaching consultations, mastermind courses, transformational classes, inspirational books, wellness retreats, and spiritual seminars—they each ended up disappointing her. But one thing they all did was inspire her to keep searching, and she signed up for more. It was a slippery slope looking for your true self, and now she was drowning in debt.

Standing in line for so long in the heat was making Joanne's back ache. A spasm of pain contorted her face, and she let out a loud, exasperated exhale between pursed lips. Just when she couldn't stand still another moment, a court officer came outside to give instructions on how to enter a federal building: two by two. His tone indicated that while he held himself in high regard, he was less than impressed with the crowd before him. His voice was gruff, and his pitch-black eyebrows were as wiry as a barbecue brush. If he ever got tired of being a court officer, he could easily be cast in a horror film with his pock-marked face and prominent teeth.

Under the watchful eye of an intimidating guard, Joanne removed her suit jacket and shoes. After she placed them in a bin, she was instructed to wait in another line to walk barefoot through the metal detector. *I hope I don't catch athlete's foot from this filthy floor.* The court officer pointed his finger at her, "You. Stay put!"

"I beg your pardon," she stuttered, looking around.

"What?"

"I need to use the ladies' room, if I may." She stood, quavering under his eye.

Having captured the undivided attention of everyone else in the foyer, he gave her a long, stony stare and snapped, "Downstairs!" Joanne grabbed her shoes and ran toward the elevator.

In the privacy of the bathroom, she could finally breathe. She washed her hands, splashed cool water on her neck and forehead, and patted them gently so as to not muss her makeup. Walking out of the ladies' room she bumped into her lawyer. She pressed her palms together in a praying gesture saying, "Thank God you're here!"

"Are you okay?"

"Yes, yes. I'm just so embarrassed!"

"Listen," he said. "There is absolutely no reason to feel embarrassed about bankruptcy. Think of it as a new beginning and not an ending." He opened the door, and they walked into a small room designated for her hearing. The air was thick with apprehension from all the cases that had gone before hers. Joanne waited for some kind of acknowledgment, but all she saw were blank stares from the five women and their lawyers sitting in the room. Joanne cast a sideways glance at them. *We're all in the same boat.*

Before she was even fully seated, her name was called. Bankruptcy court was not as she had imagined. In fact, she didn't even see a judge. Instead, a trustee had been appointed to hear her case. The trustee was tall, and although he never actually smiled, his kind hazel eyes smiled for him. After Joanne was sworn in, he began his questioning. It was over before it had hardly begun, and before she knew it, she was legally debt free.

She released a sigh so deep it defied description, originating from the core of her being. She sensed a shift inside herself and wondered if that was her soul.

REFLECTION

When you read chapter one, were you aware of how often Joanne judged people and herself?

Did you notice what triggered her judgmental thoughts?

Did Joanne's conscience bother her?

How did being judgmental have a negative effect on her physical health?

Are you judgmental? What "pushes your buttons"?

ACTION TIP

Over the next week, set a timer for one hour every day and count how often you catch yourself being judgmental.

Becoming aware of this ugly habit is the key to overcoming it.

PETITION

Dear God,

Will You please help me to stop judging other people and myself?

CHAPTER 2

Compassion

Joanne's blond curls bounced as she rushed down the front stairs of the federal building. She couldn't wait to get out of that place. With each step she took her excitement grew. Once she reached the bottom of the long staircase, a sense of exhilaration swept over her like a tidal wave. She yelled out, "Woohoo!"

Listening to the rhythm of the click-clack of her coquettish kitten heels on the pavement helped her to relax as she walked back to her car. Propelled by sheer joy, she had a buoyant spring in her step. Joanne was flying high until a bold bumble bee buzzed by and almost flew into her eye. She ducked to get out of the way. In a split second, she lost her balance and stepped on a crack in the crumbling old sidewalk. The heel of her new, beige, patent-leather shoe got stuck in the crevice, and she was stopped dead in her tracks.

She started to teeter, but as she was about to topple over, a rugged-looking man appeared out of nowhere and rescued her. Gently, he took her hands in his to steady her. He looked deep into her sparkling sky-blue eyes, and she met his gaze with a smile. She remembered him. *This is the man I prayed for this morning.* In his bloodshot, weary eyes she saw a reflection of herself, and she noticed a sense of connectedness. No fear. No judgment. When she looked at him with compassion, she recognized his addictions, his shame, his pain. *Our struggles are the same.*

Joanne rested her hand on his shoulder to balance herself as she slipped her foot out of the stuck shoe. The man grunted when he bent down to pull the heel out of the crack. As he slipped her shoe back on her foot, she was reminded of Cinderella and her prince. Just when she was about to share the analogy with him, she realized that it might give him the wrong impression, so she decided to keep that musing to herself. Deep down she knew that something magical had transpired. His compassion for her was like a key, opening the lock on her heart, and she felt God's love flow forth. She took his calloused hands and gave them a quick squeeze. "What's your name?"

"Joe."

"Thank you for helping me, Joe. My name is Joanne, but you can call me Jo."

He took a step backward and raised his shaggy black eyebrows. "We have the same name!"

Joanne noticed his trembling hands and said, "We are more alike than different."

He crammed his hands into his pockets and the color in his cheeks deepened. "What could a wretched old wreck like me have in common with a lovely young lady like you?"

"Nothing!" she bellowed and gave him a playful nudge on his shoulder. Before he could reply, she burst out laughing. "Believe me, Joe, we have a lot in common. You can't judge a book by its cover."

Joe shuffled his feet and stared at the ground, but he didn't speak right away. He wiped the sweat from his forehead with his palm and ran his hand through his fluffy, white hair. Finally, he cleared his throat and was about to say something, but Joanne jumped in.

"Sorry to interrupt—I'm dying in this heat. Want to grab some lunch?" she asked as she applied sunscreen to her freckled nose.

"Sure! My stomach is killing me, to tell you the truth. I'm not sure I ate yesterday."

"Let's go," she said, pulling her hair up with a beige silk scrunchie. "My car is down there."

"Let me guess. The fire-engine red Mercedes convertible?"

"Yup."

"Sweet," Joe said.

"Yes, it's an oldie but a goodie." Joanne smiled.

They found a parking spot on the street in front of an Italian restaurant. It had a white exterior, black shutters, and window boxes filled with cascading pink petunias. As soon as they walked in, a charming hostess seated them at a table by a large window overlooking the beautiful park across the street. She placed massive, leather-bound menus on the table. While Joanne and Joe chattered away, a waitress with a high-pitched, squeaky voice rushed up to the table and barged in on their conversation.

"Excuse me, everyone," the woman said, "I'm Toots and I will be your server. It looks like you have me all to yourselves."

"Hi, Toots!" Joanne said.

"Where is everyone today?" Joe asked.

The waitress told them she heard on the news that this July was the hottest month on record, and business was slow because people didn't want to go out in the extreme heat. Then she disappeared but returned with an ice-cold pitcher of filtered water and glasses. After pouring the water, she asked if they would like to order a cocktail. Joe looked at Joanne and gave her a sheepish grin, then they quietly chuckled at the same time and said they were fine. Joe chugged his water in one loud gulp and said, "I need to wash my hands."

Joanne chimed in, "Me too."

When they returned to the table, a basket of warm, fresh-baked Italian bread with dipping oil was waiting for them.

"Is it hard to eat with your bushy mustache?"

Joe's dense mustache wiggled when he spoke. "Not at all. I'm used to it. I've had it forever."

Joanne put her napkin on her lap, rested her elbows on the table and cupped her chin in her hands. Joe passed the bread to her.

"No, thank you."

"You're kidding, right?"

"No," she said. "I'm trying to lose a few pounds."

Joe glanced away like he was trying to think of something to say but Joanne blurted out, "After I quit smoking and drinking, I developed a new addiction—sugar."

"You? An alky?"

"Yeah, a raging alcoholic."

"What about the sugar thing?"

"I craved frosting. I used to buy birthday cakes all the time. I could never have just one piece. I had to have the whole damn cake!" She started to giggle. "Each time I ordered a cake I'd have them put a different name on it so they wouldn't know they were all for me."

Joe slapped the table and doubled over, holding his side.

"It's not funny! I gained fifty pounds!"

"So, does this mean I can eat all the bread?"

"Go for it." She grinned and passed the basket to him.

Joanne fixed her attention on Joe as he dipped a piece of crusty bread into the oil, which was mixed with parmesan cheese, chopped garlic, and crushed red-pepper flakes. His hands still trembled from his all-night drinking binge. The bread smelled so good; her mouth was watering. Having an addictive personality made it difficult for her to lose weight. She struggled with the inability to self-regulate. With hard work and discipline she did it, but now her challenge was to keep it off. Joanne placed her hand on her stomach and smiled. She only had a few more pounds to lose and didn't want to ruin all her hard work.

As soon as his bubbling lasagna arrived, Joe picked up his fork to dive in. But then he put it back down and asked Joanne if she would say grace. She closed her eyes and bowed her head.

"Come, Jesus, be our guest and let our food be blessed." Joanne plucked a cherry tomato from her salad and popped it in her mouth. "Delish!"

Joe tasted the lasagna, then fanned his mouth with his hand. "Hot!" he managed to say.

"It looks so ooey-gooey good," she cooed.

"Is that all you're going to have," Joe asked, motioning toward her salad.

"It's plenty. I just lost twenty-two pounds, and I want to keep them off." Her iPhone buzzed and she looked down to shut it off.

"Something important?"

"No, just work."

"What do you do?"

"Sell houses, teach meditation. I'm a life coach, as well."

"Perfect. You seem to be great with people."

"Thank you, Joe, and what about you?"

"I have a landscape business."

"Oh, yeah?" She glanced at his thick biceps. "That makes sense."

She started to cut her salad into bite-size pieces, then stopped. "Did you know that I saw you this morning?"

Joe blinked, picked up his water and took a long drink.

Joanne searched his face. "Around eight fifteen-ish? You were walking down the street where I parked. I was sitting in my car," she elaborated, pointing her fork in the air.

Joe stared at the lasagna on his plate. "Today is the first anniversary of my wife Kitty's death." He crossed his arms and exhaled loudly. "This morning I walked to mass to honor her memory." Joe looked down, unable to meet Joanne's eyes. "Actually, I walked because I was too wasted to drive."

Desperately, Joanne tried to find words of comfort, but all she could say was, "I am so sorry."

He took a deep breath in and held it, then he let it out and slouched. "Last night I started drinking again. Yup. I pissed away forty years of sobriety. I wanted to climb in that damn bottle of bourbon and drown myself." His cheeks flushed and he covered his face with his hands. "How is it possible to miss Kitty so much?"

Joanne didn't answer. She knew he didn't expect one. In silence, they sat together. Joe raised his hand to get the waitress's attention and pointed to the pitcher of water. Toots quickly refilled it. With shaking hands, he poured a glass of water, but much of it splashed onto the table. He guzzled the rest so fast it dribbled down his chin. He wiped his face clean with his napkin, then balled it up and threw it on his plate.

"Something really weird happened to me." He tugged at his collar, then at his ear. "I don't know if you could call it a miracle."

Joanne sat and listened, twirling her hair absently, hanging on his every word. "Go on."

He told her that as he walked to mass this morning, he felt a tingly sensation on his neck and reckoned it was prickly heat from the oppressively hot weather. Then it seemed as if a heavy weight was lifted from his shoulders and miraculously his hangover disappeared. The words of Jesus from Matthew 11:28 went through his head, "Come to me, all you who are weary, and I will give you rest."

"It was so peaceful." Joe noticed the gleam in her eyes. "What is it?"

"This just blows my mind."

Joe raised his eyebrows. "What?"

"I prayed for you this morning when you walked by my car."

"You did?"

"Yeah, and I asked God to let you know His presence and His peace."

As Joe choked back tears, he managed to say, "Thank you."

REFLECTION

As you read, did you notice how fear lost its grip on Joanne as compassion welled up from her soul?

How did compassion connect Joanne and Joe?

When was the last time you felt compassion for someone?

How did it feel?

ACTION TIP

This week, instead of criticizing someone, try to connect with them from your heart. Try to see the struggle of another person through your soul's eyes.

When you look upon someone with compassion, you become aware of God working through you.

PETITION

Dear God,

Will You please help me to see others and myself with Your compassionate eyes?

CHAPTER 3

Clarity

As Toots cleared the table, she asked if they were interested in dessert. Joanne uncrossed her ankles, put both feet on the floor, and sat up straight. "Let's take a peek?"

"You don't have to twist my arm," Joe said.

Toots came back with the menus, and in her childlike voice, she said, "I want you to know all our delectable desserts are made right here."

After Joanne glanced over the menu, she told Joe she was so glad there was nothing on it that tempted her. Toots asked what they'd decided.

"I've changed my mind," Joanne said. "Maybe I'll just have a raspberry gelato."

"And I'll have the tiramisu and a cappuccino, please."

Joanne scooted to the edge of her chair, leaned across the table, and whispered, "Joe, you are so brave to admit your slip."

Joe's eyes glazed over, and he stared out the window. He never questioned his bravery. Two tours in Vietnam had convinced him. But nothing prepared him for how brave he would have to be for Kitty in her final days on earth as cancer ravaged her body. After she passed, he didn't feel brave anymore. He wasn't afraid to admit he drank himself into oblivion last night. He was ashamed.

"Joe, what is on your mind?"

"Kitty." He paused and swallowed hard. "Even in death, her face was still beautiful. At the end, her skin was so translucent. Like, her light was radiating out through her as she was leaving this life."

They sat in silence; it was uncomfortable. Suddenly there was a loud crash and then a scream. Joanne looked at Joe, and they cracked up.

"Could that have been your tiramisu?" Joanne asked.

Just then Toots appeared with the desserts. "Here we are. Enjoy!"

When Joanne put her spoon into the flavorful gelato and took a lick, her taste buds danced with delight. Joe said his tiramisu was the best he'd ever had. It was soaked in espresso with a sweet mascarpone filling and dusted with cocoa powder. He had to hold his cappuccino cup with both hands to keep it from shaking. "This is amazing!" He leaned back in the chair and, for the first time all day, looked relaxed.

"So, Joe, tell me your story."

"Okay. I don't know where to start."

"At the beginning."

He told her how he never knew his father. His mother was an alcoholic with a split personality. Joe lived in fear, never sure if he was going to get a hug or a slug. His mother resented him and took her resentment out on him by cursing and saying he was no good. And that old tape played in his head repeatedly. All through his life he was determined to prove her wrong but couldn't because he was building his life on a negative idea. Trying to stay numb, he became addicted to alcohol.

Things started to change when he joined the army. He learned a lot about himself. He began to understand his mother and discovered that it wasn't really about him, it was always about her own lack of self-worth. She committed suicide when she was forty-six.

His life was transformed when he met Kitty. It was as if he was reborn. Every day she prayed that he could see himself and his life through God's eyes. God answered her prayers and blessed him with clarity. Joe began to see life differently. Everything became clearer the closer he got to God. He had a deep and profound conversion. His floundering landscape business began to flourish with the support of Kitty and the Twelve Steps. When they were married, her father gave them a fifty-acre estate with a private pond as a wedding gift. On the property were two vacation rental homes, each with five bedrooms and five full baths. Kitty's dad was a wealthy investor with properties all over the world. During the summer months, Kitty and Joe ran a bed and breakfast, and after Christmas, they went to Florida for the winter. They were never blessed with children. It was just the two of them, and their life was ideal for forty years. Then Kitty became sick.

After her death, a part of Joe died too. He wasn't angry with God, but he stopped giving God his time. And the further he drifted away, the less clearly he could see. He wasn't seeing from God's perspective. He wasn't feeling God's love. He was just hearing his mother's curse. His judgment got cloudy, he lost his clarity, he slipped, and he drank.

When he finished, he said, "I wonder what I was thinking last night?"

"Well, actually, Joe, you weren't thinking," she said. "You

acted on your emotions. The more intense your emotions, the more your judgment gets cloudy."

Joanne knew the pain of a relapse. It is one of the most humiliating experiences you can face regardless of the type of addiction. She remembered how it left her feeling guilty, ashamed, and ready to throw in the towel.

"Joe, that old record in your head that tells you over and over you are no good is a lie. It's not true but it did trigger something, and now it's time for you to do some serious soul searching."

"So, where do I start?"

"Get to a meeting, find someone in recovery to talk to."

"How about you?"

"You can talk to me anytime, Joe," she said, taking his hand. "Is there a meeting around here today?"

"Five o'clock," he said. "What time is it now?"

Joanne glance at her phone. "One o'clock."

"Can you give me a ride home?"

"Sure," she said. "Let's get the check."

"It's taken care of."

"How the heck did you do that?"

"When I went to wash my hands, I gave Toots my card." He smiled.

"Sneaky!"

"Yeah."

"Thank you, Joe."

Just then Toots came by with the receipt and the card. They thanked her, and as they walked toward the door, Joanne looked in her purse for her car keys. The creases in her forehead grew deeper as she dug in her purse. Joe stood by the door tapping his fingers on the front desk. A smile flashed across Joanne's face. "Viola!"

They each grabbed some mints from a crystal bowl and walked out the door. The heat hit them like a slap across the face. The sidewalk was hot enough to fry an egg, so they decided to put the top up so they wouldn't fry too.

"We go straight on Main for about a half mile. At the first set of lights, take a left; there's no sign," Joe said.

They didn't speak as they drove along the desolate country road. To avoid potholes, Joanne slowed the car. Mesmerized by the serene scenery, she felt like they had traveled back in time to another place. The brilliant green foliage of the trees banished every dark thought. Even with the top up and the air conditioner on, she detected the fragrant scent of honeysuckle. She knew it so well, and it triggered bittersweet memories—more bitter than sweet—of her childhood.

The road went up an incline, and at the top Joe said, "Stop." He got out to open a big black iron gate. Joanne viewed the spectacular beauty down below. When Joe got back in the car, he surveyed the pond and inhaled slowly. This was the place Kitty had called her piece of heaven.

Both bungalows were painted a soft white with pale blue shutters. They looked like they jumped right out of a southern architecture magazine. Wide verandas wrapped around them, and blue hydrangeas were planted across the front of each. Joe led her up the front steps, and she collapsed into a blue-floral cushioned, wicker rocking chair.

"Sit here a minute. I'll get you a cold drink."

"Water is fine, with ice, please." She sat there and looked around and listened to the soft tinkling of a wind chime. Bird songs floated in the air. In that moment, she was present. In the stillness, she said a little prayer, "God, please give Joe the clarity to see through Your eyes; let him know how much You love him."

Joe returned with the water, and she held the glass, watching the condensation. Pressing it against her forehead, she sighed, "This feels so good." She watched the ice cubes melt right before her eyes.

"Come on, I'll show you around."

Joanne looked down at her kitten heels and said, "I'll be right back. I need to get out of these shoes." She went to her car and found a pair of flip-flops in the trunk.

The backyard was a wild woodland of derelict gardens, overgrown rose bushes, broken bird baths, and birdhouses. There was a potting shed completely covered in clematis, but the trellis was collapsing. It was sad to see the neglect of such a heavenly place. The garden clearly missed Kitty as much as Joe did. The disrepair frustrated Joanne. She couldn't believe how he let this happen, and she wondered why he didn't have his landscape company take care of it as well as they did the rest of the property. Slowly it dawned on her that this was Kitty's place, and he didn't want anyone to touch it. She started to feel uncomfortable being in that space, and as if he were reading her mind, he said, "Let's go down by the pond?"

Muggy heat trickled down her back like warm soup. There wasn't a breath of air so she said, "Yes, maybe it will feel cooler down near the water."

He led her down a narrow path; on the right was rickety old split-rail fence that bordered the trail all the way to the pond. It was completely covered with jasmine, and Joanne couldn't find a spot to place her hand to steady herself on the path. The intoxicating scent put her in a heady trance. Watching the hummingbirds, butterflies, and honeybees search for the sweet nectar held her spellbound. Unfortunately, the spell was abruptly broken when she slipped and landed on her fanny. As Joe bent over to help her up, his mustache softly brushed her ear, and a swoony sensation came over her. She let out a small gasp, letting go of his hand as if it were a hot potato. Self-consciously, she stood and brushed the prickly pine needles off her behind.

As they continued, a barn on top of a hill became visible through the trees, and they came upon a beautiful meadow. Purple and blue wildflowers bowed in the breeze, cascading down the grassy slope. At the bottom was an idyllic spot for the picnic tables, benches, and Adirondack chairs someone had placed there years ago. As they approached, she saw ducks swimming in a small pond. "Oh my gosh, Joe!" she said. "Lily pads!"

Joe said, "And if you look really hard, you might even see a frog."

She squinted. "There's one. It's sitting on that leaf."

"Yeah. Sit over here, and if you listen carefully, you can hear them croaking." Joe motioned her over to a small, weather-beaten bench under a weeping willow. Quiet enveloped them as they sat, shaded by the graceful tree. Listening to the leaves rustling in the gentle breeze was so peaceful. Joanne didn't want to leave, but she had a nagging feeling she was in Kitty's seat. She closed her eyes, inhaled, and let that image go from her mind, forcing herself to stay present.

She looked at Joe. "There is a sacredness here. It transcends all my worries and concerns."

"Yes. Sometimes I can feel the breath of God."

"Joe, this is a great place to heal."

"Uh-huh."

After a moment, she continued. "Is there a grief support group at your church?"

Joe mused, "Probably."

"Why don't you check it out?"

He kicked at the grass and released an impatient huff.

"Joe, you know things are never going to be the same. You have to go on living. Grief is like a fog. You can't see the beauty of life in front of you until the sun shines through and evaporates the clouds. Only then do you get clarity."

Joe picked up a pebble and threw it in the pond. They watched the ripples spreading out.

Joanne pointed to the ripples. "Our lives are like that pebble in the pond; we create ripples of change. What kind of change could you make possible for yourself and others if you make your way through the fog?"

Joe scratched his head and asked, "What do you mean?"

"Your actions can have far reaching effects. How many people will be inspired, touched, or changed by you?"

Looking at her sideways, Joe responded with a shrug of his shoulders.

"Well, perhaps God has more for you to do."

"You think?" He paused for the space of a heartbeat. "Like what?"

Joanne motioned out toward the pond. "Like making positive ripples with your life."

"That's easy for you to say, Jo. You've got a bright and bubbly personality like no one else I know. But I'm an introvert."

"Tonight, at the meeting, if anyone asks you to be their sponsor, just agree. You would be wonderful, and it's a way for you to make positive ripples." She smiled and her eyes sparkled.

"It's funny you should say that. Kitty was always after me to be a sponsor."

"Well, we'd better get going," Joanne said. In the distance she saw a faded blue swing hanging motionless from the bough of a huge oak tree. It almost seemed to be calling to her. With unabashed glee, she ran toward it. Her hands reached up to take hold of the frayed ropes, but the bough creaked, startling her. Nevertheless, she pushed her feet against the dirt and up she went. Holding tight to the coarse rope, she pumped her legs, closed her eyes, and enjoyed the sensation of floating. In her mind she saw the little girl she once had been, and her eyes teared a bit at the memory of her self-inflicted wounds. *I am sorry, please forgive me.* She thought she heard a gentle voice in her head say "Hush!" but quickly dismissed the notion. Then a lightning bolt of an idea flashed across her mind. In bold letters the word "VALUABLE" appeared. It was so sharp, so clear. A rush of excitement overcame her, and when she jumped off the swing, she fell on the ground.

Joe came running over. "You okay?"

"I'm better than okay. I am valuable, and you are too."

"What are you talking about?" he said, brushing dirt off of her.

"God sees you as valuable. He sent His only son Jesus to earth to die for you. That's how valuable you are. That's how much He loves you."

Joe stared at Joanne with his eyes wide open. He was at a loss for words.

Joanne said, "Just now, I saw the word "VALUABLE" written across my mind. I know it was a divine message."

A faucet of grief opened, gushing salty tears down Joe's face. "Kitty used to say that," he sobbed into his hands.

She could see there would be no closing the floodgates. "Joe, just have yourself a good cry." Watching him in pain and sorrow was breaking her heart, but she knew she couldn't help. She began to cry, too, and then she prayed. When she reached out to put her hands on his shoulders, he recoiled against her touch, wailing even louder. After a few minutes, the tears subsided.

Joe spoke in a cracking voice, "I know Kitty wants me to get on with my life," he sniffled and wiped his nose with his sleeve.

Joanne said, "God does too."

He looked at her with his sad, red eyes and mumbled, "I just wish I knew how."

"Don't worry. He's going to show you the way. When you're ready."

Letting out a long, loud exhale, Joe said "I have to take a quick shower before we go to the meeting."

"Good idea. I can wait on the veranda. But may I use your guest bathroom first?"

"Follow me."

Joanne's eyes popped when she saw the glossy grand piano sitting center stage in the living room.

"Wow!" she blurted. "Do you play?"

"I used to play every day for Kitty, but I haven't touched the darn thing since …" Joe made a huffing sound and abruptly turned and disappeared down the hall. Joanne sensed a longing as she stood in the foyer, staring blankly at Joe walking away.

After Joanne freshened up, she walked back out onto the veranda and settled into a rocking chair. Watching the clouds roll by had a hypnotic effect on her, and in no time, she dozed off.

The sound of classical music awakened her. The melody floated in the humid air and drew her into the house to see Joe playing the piano. Her eyes glistened when she saw the look on his face and felt the music beating in his heart.

"I forgot how therapeutic it is to play," he said as he looked up. Joanne walked over closer to him and watched in rapt attention as his fingers glided over the keys. Overwhelmed with emotion, she held her breath as the music washed over her.

Joe turned from the piano. "At the end, hospice had set this room up as a bedroom for Kitty. Because she was dying, she refused to call it the living room anymore. So, we agreed to just call it the piano room. When she died," he paused for a moment. "When she died, the music died too. Thank you for bringing it back to life."

"It wasn't me, Joe. It was God." Her heart swelled with gratitude, and she murmured, "Thank You, God."

REFLECTION

Did you notice how grief clouded Joe's perception?

Have you experienced a challenging situation that clouded your perception? Did it seem hopeless? What was the outcome?

God gives us all our trials for a reason. What did you learn about yours?

ACTION TIP

Renew your relationship with God by starting a daily routine of spending time with Him. Every day at the same time, set a timer for ten minutes and simply sit in His presence. Just be with Him. Ask Him to give you clarity. Ask Him to open the eyes to your heart. Then sit with Him and listen.

Journaling is another way to develop your relationship with God. When you journal every day at the same time, you will be amazed at how your day improves. Whenever you are confused, writing about the problem gives you clarity. Set a timer for ten minutes and write to God about anything that is on your mind. Just write to Him.

Deborah O'Brien

PETITION

Dear God,

Can You please bless me with the gift of clarity so I can see from Your point of view?

CHAPTER 4

Honesty

Dread filled Joanne as she drove into the parking lot. It had been a long time since she'd attended an AA meeting, kind of like when you haven't been to church in a long time. A twinge of guilt upset her stomach.

"Ugh!" Joanne said with an exasperated sigh. She shut the car off and looked at Joe. "Are you ready?"

"Heck no!" he said. "I could barf right now."

"Me too. Oh well, here we go anyway."

As soon as they walked in the door, Joe received a warm welcome. The guy who was busy making coffee called him over. "Hey, Joe!" he said, giving him a bear-sized hug. "Missed you!"

"Thanks, Al."

Al gave Joe a clap on his back and winked. "Who's that cutie-pie?"

"Um … just a friend."

Al winked and gave the okay sign. "Listen, can you do me a huge favor?"

"Depends."

"Our guest speaker for tonight just canceled. Can you run the meeting for me?"

Joe grimaced and shuffled his feet. "I'm so embarrassed. It's just been too long."

Al leaned close to Joe, so close he could smell the coffee on his breath. "Look, Joe, no one here has forty-years sobriety."

Joe moaned, "I can't."

Al nudged him with his elbow. "Sure you can. You're a legend in your own time."

Joe tugged on his mustache and said, "Okay."

Al gave him a pat on the back. "Thanks, buddy!"

As Joe approached Joanne, she could see fear written all over his face. "What's up?"

"I don't know how he talked me into it." Joe scratched his head. "One minute he was giving me a friendly hug," he continued, his eyes wide in disbelief, "and the next thing I knew, I agreed to speak tonight."

"Good!" she said. Joanne's whole face lit up when she smiled at him. Her dimples got deeper right before his eyes.

"I have to sit over there," he pointed.

"No problem."

There was a semi-circle of fold-up chairs. Joe sat in the middle tapping his Ray-Bans on a tiny table.

Joanne glanced around to find a place to sit and noticed a few people shifting uncomfortably in their chairs as though they didn't want to be there. Perhaps a judge ordered them to attend this meeting. A lot of people walk into a meeting for the first time with a chip on their shoulder, but as the saying goes, one day at a time they begin to heal. Maybe in a month from now some of these people will walk out with a chip in their hand to acknowledge their sobriety.

She parked herself on the end and gave a nervous grin to the girl next to her. The girl scowled and slouched in her seat.

The smell of the room was so familiar. She wondered if all AA halls smelled the same, like a mix of perspiration and desperation with a hint of stale cigarettes and old coffee. She wrinkled her nose and sniffed. There was another odor. She recognized it right away. It was the unmistakable scent of a woman on a hot day. *I hope that's not me.*

After Joanne got sober, she developed a heightened sense of smell. She hadn't decided if it was a curse or a blessing. Tonight it was really annoying! Her nose was assaulted by yet another stinky smell. She was certain it wasn't her, but to make sure, she raised her right arm and, pretending to wave to an imaginary person in the back of the room, she stuck her nose into her armpit and took a long inhalation. *Well, at least my deodorant is holding up.* She winced when she tried to run her fingers through her hair. *It's a rat's nest. I am a mess.* Slowly, she turned her head and took a sneak peek at the girl next to her. Telltale wet rings circled the armpits of her pretty pink blouse. *Oh, my goodness! She must be a wreck.*

Realizing she was obsessing about all the smells as a way to escape guilt, she was ashamed to admit she had not been to a meeting in over a year. She knew she was reverting to her old patterns. She had to stop the "stinkin' thinkin'."

Joe started the meeting by reading the "AA Preamble," then he led the group in the "Serenity Prayer." After everyone had a chance to introduce themselves, he said, "Hello. My name is Joe, and I am an alcoholic."

In unison, the entire group responded, "Hi, Joe."

"Some of you know me as the old timer with forty years of sobriety under my belt." He leaned on the table to brace himself. In a low, gravelly voice he said, "Last night I almost drank myself to death."

He coughed to clear his throat and paused to look around the room. His face turned beet red. "I am powerless over alcohol and my life has become unmanageable," he spoke haltingly. "Today I'm a newcomer, just like you." He pointed to a few of the first timers. "I need to be here; I need to be with you. The one thing to remember—the one thing never to forget—dishonesty kills alcoholics. So be honest with everyone and be honest with yourself."

And then he told his story. No one fidgeted in their seats, they were all riveted on him. When he finished, he opened the meeting for everyone to have a chance to speak. At the end they formed a circle and held hands as they prayed the Lord's Prayer.

After the meeting, Al came over and shook Joe's hand. "Great job. You are an inspiration."

"Thanks, Al. It's good to be back."

Joanne watched from a distance as Joe interacted with the group. She couldn't believe this was the same man she saw stagger by her car this morning. Despite his age and his white hair, she could see the boy in him. His mind was sharp, his body was lean, and the beauty of his soul shined from his eyes for everyone to see.

As they got up to leave, the girl who was so stand-offish with the sizable scowl turned to Joanne with a sweet smile and gave her a sweaty hug. "Great meeting, huh?"

"Yes!"

"Doesn't Joe look just like that old-time cowboy actor? What's his name?"

"You mean Sam Elliot?"

"That's the one."

"Now that you mention it, he does!"

She offered a timid handshake and said, "My name is Diane. Want to, um, grab a coffee sometime?"

"Hi, I'm Joanne. Here's my card. Call me and we can make a plan."

"Oh my God!" she said as she looked at the card. "You're a meditation teacher? I've been wanting to learn."

"Well, now you can."

She shrugged and walked away, and Joanne regarded her reflectively for a moment. She was happy Diane took off her hostility mask; she reminded Joanne of herself, and she recalled her own early days in AA when she wore a hostility mask to hide her apprehension. After many years of discipline and determination she finally learned how to take off the mask and be honest with herself. When Joanne was just a little girl, her mother used to tell her all the time that she was a born liar, and Joanne believed it. The hardest habit she ever had to break was lying to herself. And that wasn't easy. To quit lying takes strong character and, let's be honest, liars don't have that quality. Joanne found journaling was the best tool for combating her self-deception and building her character. Just like she couldn't eat one potato chip or have one drink or have one piece of cake, she couldn't tell one lie because once she started, she couldn't stop.

A sense of gratitude overcame her. *Thank You, Lord, for getting me here.* Wandering through the crowd, she glanced over at Joe and he beamed. She felt that flutter in her stomach again. *Stop it, stop it, stop it right now! What is wrong with you? He is old enough to be your father!*

A small crowd gathered around Joe. Standing there in his eye-catching magenta polo shirt and indigo jeans, he radiated a sense of calm self-confidence and authenticity. Although he didn't like being put in the limelight, his charismatic personality made him a magnet, drawing people to him. He possessed the gift of being able to put people at ease. Joanne watched him and wondered if it was his smooth, smoky voice or his nonchalant manner that made everyone relax around him. One thing she knew for sure, he didn't wear a mask. *He is the real thing.* She gave her full attention to not only what he said, but what he didn't say and the way he listened carefully to what others had to say. Listening to the sound of his deep, resonant voice was soothing to her soul.

Joe motioned to the door and gave Joanne a Cheshire-cat grin. She realized he was ready to go, but something in his eyes made her knees weak, so she looked in her purse for her car keys to avoid his gaze. She pulled them out, got on her tip toes, held the keys up high over her head, and let them jangle. Then she gave Joe a quick half smile and an exaggerated wink. *I can't believe I did that!* Automatically, her right hand went to her suprasternal notch and she shuddered.

A sudden urgency to urinate overcame her. She had to go so bad she was afraid she might wet her pants right there. When she walked into the ladies' room, she was surprised to see all the stalls were empty and the place was clean. Two sexy femme fatales were chatting in front of the mirror and blocking the way (breaking the bathroom etiquette rules). As she squeezed by, she couldn't help noticing they were poured into tight, butt-boosting jeans.

Joanne rushed into the first stall (her aunt told her to never use the middle stall). She didn't mean to eavesdrop on the conversation, but when she heard "Joe," it got her attention. She stopped her pee in midstream and strained to listen, but with the deafening whirling sound of the bathroom fan, it was difficult to hear. At first, she heard a shrill cackling followed by hushed babbling, and then as clear as crystal, she heard, "Grief is nature's most powerful aphrodisiac."

Joanne stifled a gasp.

"A romp in the hay is just what he needs to straighten him out."

"He does have a nice barn. Mwah-ha-ha!"

Joanne came out of the stall. The dynamic duo were still snickering when they noticed her. They tried to stop, and one made a snorting noise. *How apropos.*

While Joanne was washing her hands, she heard, "Hey, I love the color of your hair. Where do you go?"

After Joanne dried her hands, she took a card out of her wallet and gave it to her. "Ask for Bobbie Jo, the owner of the Salon at Stonecroft."

"Thanks," the woman said, staring at Joanne with huge green eyes that peered out from under long, blond bangs that were overdue for a trim.

Her friend asked, "Do you suppose she could help me?"

"Of course!"

She leaned over and revealed two inches of gray roots that were screaming, "Cover me!" Her eyes were different, one brown and one yellow, and she had an exotic look.

There was something about these two women. Joanne couldn't put her finger on it, but she knew. She could see it in their eyes. They were bewitching and a little bit scary. As she headed for the door, the taller one said, "Hey, what's your name?"

"Joanne."

"I'm Delilah and this is Dahlia. Nice to meet you!"

"Thanks." *I'll have to warn Joe about those two. I bet those aren't their real names.*

REFLECTION

Joanne struggled with lying. Do you tend to lie? Think about it. Even little white lies are harmful.

Being honest takes practice. Have you been caught in a lie lately? What did you learn?

ACTION TIP

Set the timer for five minutes and start writing about what honesty means to you. Keep writing about why you want to be honest. Why is it important to you? Write in your journal every day.

During the day, try to keep track of how many slips you made. You will find so many of those little white lies were unnecessary, and you will feel the freedom of telling the truth.

Challenge yourself to improve every day, and when you slip, forgive yourself and start all over again.

PETITION

Dear God,

I am so sorry for all the times I have been dishonest. Help me to be honest with myself and everyone I meet.

CHAPTER 5

Respond

A small crowd gathered around Joe, making it difficult for him to leave the meeting. When he finally got to the car, Joanne was sitting there with the top down. He hopped in and said, "Ready?"

"Uh-huh."

Just as she put the car in drive, out of nowhere a wiry guy with unruly blond hair jumped in front of them, forcing Joanne to slam on the brakes. The young man proceeded to pound his fist on the hood of her car, yelling, "Stop!"

A chorus of four-letter words exploded from Joe.

Joanne leaped out of the car and lurched toward the stranger, screaming, "You idiot!"

Joe got out of the car and said, "Calm down, everyone."

Joanne folded her arms across her chest and said through gritted teeth, "I better not see any dents in that hood."

Joe looked the hood over, assuring her it was fine, but Joanne sucked in a deep breath and threw her arms in the air. The guy flinched. He looked like he wanted to run for the hills, and he nervously checked his phone.

"Put that thing away when I'm talking to you." She put her face close to his and gave him a little poke. "You asshole! You just scared ten years off my life!"

"Hey! Back up, lady, you're in my space. You're the scary one. I just need to talk to Joe." He kicked her tire, stepped away and looked at Joe. "I hate to get off on the wrong foot, Joe. My name is Zack. I wanted to ask if you'd be my sponsor. I was just afraid you guys would take off before I had a chance." His striking glacier-blue, but ice-cold, eyes were pleading. "They say to stick with the winners, and that would be you, Joe." He handed Joe a piece of paper with his name and number scribbled on it.

Joe took the slip of paper. "Look. Jack—"

"Zack."

"Right. Sorry. Zack, let's talk tomorrow night after the meeting."

"Thanks," he said as he tossed his sun-bleached blond hair back with a flip of his head, nodded at Joanne, and swaggered away.

"Looks like the only job he has this summer is working on his tan."

Joe raised an eyebrow. "Joanne, didn't you tell me 'You can't judge a book by its cover.'"

"Sure, but did you see his eyes? Killer eyes. They scared me."

"You sure as hell didn't appear scared. You looked like you were going to knock his lights out." Joe opened the car door for her, and as she lowered herself in, her face turned as red as the leather bucket seats.

She looked down to avoid his eyes. "I'm embarrassed that I reacted like that. That guy triggered something in me, and I lost control. You must think I'm a lunatic."

"Yeah, but a cute one," Joe said with a grin that couldn't be contained.

"Seriously, Joe. He seems like a wild card. Totally unpredictable."

"Oh. And you're not?"

"Well …" Joanne tried to defuse the situation. "But I'm cute!"

"This is a perfect example of what Jesus spoke against—hypocritical judging. He didn't just say, 'Don't judge.' He commanded it! Why? Because he couldn't stand hypocrites. Hypocritical judging is when we find fault with others and overlook our own faults.

"Let's face it, Joanne, you were being judgmental. Before you criticize Zack, look at your own actions. You were screaming at him like a wild banshee. Then to add fuel to the fire, you got right in his face and tried to provoke him. I saw you poke him with your finger. Remember, anytime you point a finger at someone, you have three fingers pointing back at you."

"I know. It was stupid. I was wrong not to respond. I should have just paused before I spoke."

"And taken a deep breath."

"And taken a deep breath," she repeated. "I'm addicted to reacting, it's like a power over me … all the drama."

"You can break that habit. Next time you find yourself about to react, take a deep breath, pause, and ask God for His perspective. Then you can respond with responsibility."

"How'd you get to be so smart?"

"Heck, I'm guilty too." Joe smiled. "When I saw Zack all dressed in black, my first inkling was a ninja surprise attack. Did you notice that scar on his face?"

"No! Where was it?"

"It must have been six inches down his left cheek."

Joanne put her hand up to her own cheek, letting out a small gasp. "Imagine getting slashed in the face. The horror of it!"

"Imagine being scarred for life?"

"Yes, I can," she said as she started the car.

"Joanne, shut the car off, please." He reached over and took her hand off the steering wheel. Gently, he turned her hand over. He looked long and hard at the jagged scar on her wrist. As he took a deep inhale, she groaned and stared straight ahead. "Do you want to talk about this?" Joe asked.

"This? This is the result of reacting instead of responding."

Joe sighed, giving Joanne a quizzical look. "Do you want to tell me about it?"

"It's a long story."

"I have time."

"But I don't, Joe. Not today. I need to get home. After I drop you off, I have to get on the road." She put the car in reverse, revved the engine, and said, "Come on. I'm gonna take you on a joyride." She popped the car into drive.

"Mind if I turn the radio on?" Joe asked.

"Go ahead."

Joe was flipping through the channels when he heard a song he liked. A low, hoarse sound came from deep inside him as he leaned his head back on the headrest and closed his eyes. The music and the words to the song stirred Joanne as well. Emotions welled up inside of her, and she, too, was quiet. Turning the volume up, they drove along, feeling the rush of the wind and the rush of something else … After the song was over, he shut the radio off, and they drove the rest of the way in silence.

When they arrived at the compound, she parked in front of

the first house, and Joe turned to her. "Thanks for the ride—for the whole day."

"Yeah. It was … very … nice," she whispered.

"Can I have your card?"

Joanne snatched one from her center console and handed it to him with a lusty laugh. "I just happen to have one right here."

"Thanks." He smiled, taking it from her hand.

They stared at each other until she was able to stammer, "Bye-bye."

Joe got out of the car and walked around to her side. Leaning on her door he said, "This is not the end, it's just the beginning."

A tingly chill went up her spine. "You know, Joe, my lawyer said the exact same words this morning."

"Drive safe." Joe patted her car door.

As she put the top up on the car, she took one more long look at Joe. "Too-da-loo!" she yelled out the window as she drove off.

Joe stood in the driveway watching her until she disappeared from sight. Then he bent over and put his hands on his thighs, trying to catch his breath. *She takes my breath away.* Slowly he climbed the steps to the porch and called out, "God, please help me," into the quiet evening.

REFLECTION

> Being able to respond takes clarity. Before you react, pause and breathe. Joanne did not consider the consequences. Does this ever happen to you? Do you react instead of respond? Next time you feel the pressure to react, try to identify the triggers.

ACTION TIP

Make a commitment to practice responding this week. Each time you feel as if you may lose your temper, just pause and breathe. Make a few consistent decisions to stop reacting every day.

Each morning, write in your calendar: Today I intend to respond and not react. Make an intention each day.

At night, before you go to sleep, review your day.

PETITION

Dear God,

Please forgive me for all the times I have reacted and made a mess of things. I am truly sorry. Can You please help me to learn how to respond in all situations?

CHAPTER 6

Charity

As she drove home, she hummed the song. She couldn't get the words out of her head. They touched her in spots so raw and deep. Secret places she didn't want to go. Dark memories of violent moments flooded her mind and crashed down like angry waves on a stormy night; visions of drowning in sorrow, drowning in booze, drowning in a bloody bathtub, drowning in debt. And now she couldn't breathe. She was drowning in negativity.

To stop the tormenting thoughts in her head, she popped a CD into the player and engaged her heart by singing along with the spiritual songs. The music lifted her to new heights of awareness, and her soul soared. Out loud she prayed, *Thank You, dear God.*

It was almost nine o'clock when she arrived home. After she futzed around her apartment for a while, she took a seat at her desk and mustered the energy to scan all her messages. There was a text from Joe, *Are you home yet?* As she read it, she perceived a faint flutter in her tummy. A tiny laugh bubbled out of her, and she texted him an emoji smiling face.

It occurred to her that she didn't have dinner. *Humph, I'll have a late-night snack.* She took out her crystal-footed, tulip sundae dish and placed in it a generous scoop of vanilla ice cream. On top, she drizzled an itsy-bitsy amount of caramel sauce. Just as she sank into her yellow curvilinear chair, she heard the phone, but she ignored it. Instead, she propped her feet up on the ottoman, kicked off her shoes, and dug into the ice cream with her long-handled spoon. *Yummo!* One bite was all it took. All was right with her world.

She toppled into bed, too tired to wash her face. Every night before she fell asleep, she named five things she was grateful for. Tonight, she prayed, *I am grateful to be debt free, to get off the hamster wheel, to get a new lease on life, to be healthy, and to get another second chance.* A smile escaped her lips despite her weariness, and she said, *Thank You, dear God, for putting Joe on my path.*

Joanne enjoyed a sense of freedom working part-time in real estate. It gave her some income, and it allowed her to pursue her passion for life coaching and teaching meditation. The problem was that she worked around the clock, but she didn't earn enough money. Now, in the stillness of the night, she speculated on how to fit Joe into her hectic schedule. *Something's gotta give.* As soon as she let go of the control, she went out like a light.

Up at the crack of dawn, Joanne stood on her balcony watching the sun peek over the horizon. It seemed to speak to her soul, saying "Welcome to the first day of your new beginning." While she sipped coffee and enjoyed the breeze, she was mesmerized by all the hues that filled the sky. Today, soft streaks of melon pink, peach orange, lemon yellow, rhubarb purple, and watermelon red reminded her of yummy flavors of sherbet. All of a sudden, she was ravenous. After she gobbled down a protein bar, she licked her fingers clean. When she attempted to stuff the crumpled wrapper into her bathrobe pocket, she found something else was there. She reached in, and to her surprise, she pulled out a crisp one-hundred-dollar bill. She let out a squeal and held the bill with both hands in front of her. *Where did you come from?* She racked her brain but couldn't understand how the money got into her pocket. As she spun in a wild circle, waving the money in the air, Joanne did a happy dance. Looking up at the sky, she said, *Thank You, God!* She curled up on her chaise longue, grabbed her journal from the side table, and began to write.

Joanne had her alarm set for six fifteen each morning, and she would spend fifteen minutes reading her daily inspiration from her devotional and Bible. In her bedroom walk-in closet there was a chair where she sat quietly in prayer and meditation. Joanne had a daily routine of spending the first hour of her day in God's presence. Someone had suggested it to her at a retreat she'd attended ten years ago. It was the best advice she'd ever received, and she believed this practice had transformed her life. Now in the quiet of her heart He spoke, and she was filled with peace. Throughout the day, nothing would be able to steal her inner calm. No matter what happened, she would have the strength to handle it without falling apart. When she let go and let God orchestrate her day, it flowed.

However, on the days when she got up late and didn't have time for Him, all hell would break loose; she would rush around like a chicken with its head cut off, trying to get everything under control, but it would end up helter-skelter.

Just as she was about to step into the shower, she heard the phone, but she couldn't find it. *Where is that darn thing?* She spotted it buried under some papers on her messy desk. Her heart raced as she rushed to answer it, but she was seconds too late. Placing her glasses on her nose, she saw Joe's name on the screen. She pressed "call back," but it rang and rang and rang with no answer. She left a quick message, "Hi, Joe. Sorry I missed your call. Can you call me back?"

After a quick shower, Joanne got ready lickety-split and was off and running to get to her first appointment on time. As she was driving, her phone rang, and she grabbed it without checking the display so she wouldn't take her eyes off the road. "Hi there!" she said, trying to sound bubbly.

"Joanne?" It was Joe. Her heart skipped a beat.

"Yes, it's me."

"I, um, I'll make this quick. How about dinner tomorrow night?"

"I would love to."

"It's a date. I'll call you tonight at eight."

"Okey dokey. And, Joe, have a good day."

"Thanks. You too."

When she ended the call, she screamed for joy, "It's a date!" *Better put away those happy thoughts to savor later. It's show time.*

Driving up the driveway to the open house, she couldn't help but speculate. *This place is going to sell itself with such great curb appeal.*

Joanne struggled to get the cumbersome open house sign out of her car. *I wish someone was here to help me with this darn thing.* She sank the super-sized sign into the ground and pushed her blond curls from her face, letting out an impatient huff. Last week Joanne staged the house, and yesterday someone from the office placed fresh flowers on the kitchen counter. Now all she had to do was bake some chocolate chip cookies to give the house a homey aroma.

Just as she placed the cookie dough in the oven, a question popped into her head. *Where did you put the dough you found this morning?* She pulled out her wallet and opened it up. The one-hundred-dollar bill wasn't there, and her heart sank. Her brow furrowed as she tried to recall. Her mind raced at all the possibilities. She bit her lip and looked around as if it would somehow magically reappear. *Did you leave it on the balcony to blow away? That's just like you. You blow money away. No wonder you never have any.* She wanted to leave and look for the money, but she couldn't go. People would be arriving any minute. *Oh no! The cookies!* She got them out of the oven just as the doorbell rang. She walked into the foyer praying, *St. Anthony, St. Anthony, come around, come around, my money is lost, and it must be found.* Opening the door, she greeted the people with a cheerful smile and a friendly welcome while the delicious smell of homemade cookies wafted into the foyer.

When the open house ended a few hours later, Joanne collapsed into a chair and let out a sigh of relief. Closing her eyes for a moment, she was startled by the ring of her cell phone. It was Greg from the real estate office.

"Hi."

"How'd it go?"

"It didn't. Only two lookie-loos all morning."

"Bummer."

"You bet."

"Chin up, maybe this afternoon. What time is the next one?"

"Three to five."

"Go get 'em, tiger."

"Yup. Thanks, Greg." One after another defeatist thought began to parade through Joanne's mind but halted abruptly when she heard herself scream, "Stop obsessing!"

For a moment she sat still and surveyed the room. She heard a buzzing sound in her head. Looking down, she noticed her hands resting limp in her lap. For the first time, she was fully aware of all the colors in the floral pattern of her new sundress. Yellows, reds, pinks, purples, and shades of orange, too. *Wow! They are the same as the yummy colors of the sunrise this morning.* She smiled, remembering the day she bought the dress. When she took it off the rack, the saleslady said, "Gotta try that one on. It's perky, just like you."

"I'll take it." As she strutted out of the store, the saleslady hollered out to her, "That dress will keep your spirit high."

Now, focusing her attention on all the colors on her lap, she sensed her vibrations rise, and she murmured "That saleslady was right." Immediately Joanne stood up, smoothed her dress, and flounced out of the house.

On her way home, she stopped at the ice cream parlor. Bouncing on her toes at the counter, she said, "I'll have a small raspberry sherbet on a sugar cone, please." When she took a lick, she smacked her lips and muttered, "Mmm!"

Driving along, Joanne started to speculate about the money. *I bet you put it back in your bathrobe pocket, right where you found it.* First thing she did when she arrived home was run into the bathroom and pull her pink chenille bathrobe off the hook. Holding her breath, she stuffed her small fist into the pocket, but nothing was there. She let out a shallow sigh and tried the other pocket. When she felt the crisp paper, her eyes lit up and she shouted, "Eureka!" Pulling it out, she almost cried. It was the crinkled wrapper of the protein bar. Sagging against the wall, she gripped her robe and buried her face in the soft, fuzzy chenille. Joanne drew in slow, steady breaths. *Retrace your steps.*

She opened the door to the balcony and was met with a blast of heat, which took her by surprise. She stepped back into the air-conditioned room to rack her brain. With her hands on her hips and a pout on her face, she stood there looking out. As her eyes were ping-ponging all over the space, she began to get a headache. Her focus fell on the little table. *I bet it's in my journal.* Joanne jerked at the drawer but couldn't open it. High humidity was the culprit, causing the wood to swell. She yelled, "Oh this darn icky-sticky weather!" Then she ran back into the apartment and came out with her blow dryer. Aiming the heat at the drawer, she was slowly able to get rid of the moisture and open the drawer. "Phew!" She grabbed the journal and flipped through the pages. But the money wasn't there.

Dripping sweat from head to toe, she raced inside to get a drink of water and tripped over her green Bible lying on the floor. She wondered what it was doing there. As she bent down to pick it up, she had a flash of intuition. She knew the money was tucked in the Bible. Picking it up, she flipped through it, and there the money was—being used as a bookmark to the scripture she had read in the morning. In her hurry to read the inspiration it went in one ear and out the other. *I have to stop rushing around.* A flush crept across her face. Embarrassment stole the elation of finding the money. With a heavy hollowness in her chest and a lump in her throat, she sat in her closet and prayed, *Oh, dear God, please forgive me for being so careless with that money, for rushing around and not focusing. Please, Lord, help me to be present in all that I do. Help me to pay attention starting with You. I love You.*

She closed her eyes, and warm tears spilled out just a few at a time. She experienced a floating sensation, like all her burdens had been removed. In that present moment, her soul was filled with the love of God. Making the sign of the cross, she softly whispered, "Thank You."

When Joanne filled out a deposit slip, she noticed a tiny tingling in her fingers. *What is that?* Just as she was about to put the money and the deposit slip in an envelope, she stopped to stare at the image of Ben Franklin on the bill. She wondered how one man accomplished so much. She googled him and read that he scheduled everything in his life. Scheduling was the secret to his success. Every morning he would ask, "What good shall I do today?" And in the evening, before he would go to sleep, he would ask, "What good have I done today?" Joanne decided to take his advice, went on Amazon, and ordered his book.

While she was brushing her teeth, she began to daydream about the things she would like to buy with the money. *Stop it right now! You have to change your way of thinking.* Clutching the envelope, she recalled the words her mother said to her when she was a little girl, "Money burns a hole in your pocket." *Today is a new beginning.*

With her arms swinging back and forth, Joanne marched up to the counter at her local bank. The teller said, "I love your dress. You look like a ray of sunshine today."

Joanne glowed with appreciation. "Aw, thanks, Jennette. Hey, congratulations! I heard about your promotion. I'm so proud of you."

"Thank you. And what can I do for you today?"

Joanne tapped the envelope on the counter. "Deposit, please." Then she let out a loud, "Ow!" Her eyes were wide as she spun around to see who kicked her. There stood a frantic mother clutching the grimy little hand of her squirming young son. *What a brat.*

Hiding a black eye behind her lifeless brown hair, the frail mother kept her eyes on the child as she apologized. "Did he hurt you?"

"No, no, I'm fine. Why don't you go ahead of me?" As Joanne stepped aside, she squeezed her eyes shut to erase a picture in her mind of herself with the same swollen face and the same sense of shame. Her stomach turned sour. Without any warning, vomit came up and stuck in her throat.

She flew into the ladies' room. After she washed her mouth and splashed water on her face, she flopped down on a bench and tried to steady her breath. In no time at all she was revived. As she sat there, she remembered that she had a gift certificate to McDonalds tucked in her handbag. Something in the boy's sullen eyes tugged at her heart strings. *I bet he would love a Happy Meal.*

Coming out of the ladies' room, she caught a glimpse of the mother and child leaving the bank. Waving the gift card in the air, she rushed to catch up with them. "Yoo-hoo!" she yelled. "Wait up!"

When the young mother turned around, Joanne handed her the card. "Enjoy this please. I can't use it. I'm on a diet."

Despite her black and blue eye, her bruised cheek, and her chipped front teeth, the woman smiled and said, "God bless you."

Joanne ran her tongue over her own chipped front tooth, and in that split second their souls connected. Joanne took the one-hundred-dollar bill out of the envelope and placed it in the young mother's hand. "This is for you," she said, and her eyes glowed with inner light.

REFLECTION

> Did you notice how happy Joanne felt to be able to give to the mother and son? Can you remember a time when you felt the joy of giving? It is amazing how giving can lift your spirit. Anytime you can lift another soul, you benefit.

ACTION TIP

Find ways you can help someone you know. Mother Teresa said, "If you can't feed a hundred people, then feed just one."

Whenever you give, somehow it always comes back to you. Try to follow Ben Franklin's advice. Every morning ask yourself, "What good can I do today?" At night before you go to bed ask again, "What good have I done today?" Make an intention to give every day. It doesn't have to be money. You can give of yourself, your attention, your time, your talent.

Think about it. What can you give today?

PETITION

Dear God,

Thank You for blessing me so abundantly. Please help me to be generous. Please help me to be aware of others in need. I pray that I can be charitable in my thoughts, words, and deeds. Use me for Your glory.

CHAPTER 7

Mercy

It was almost eight o'clock. While Joanne waited to hear from Joe, she nestled into her comfy chair and sat there crossing and uncrossing her legs as she doodled circles, stars, and hearts all over her notebook. When her cell phone rang, she grabbed for it, knocking over her water bottle.

"Darn!" she yelled. Then in a high-pitched, animated voice she answered her phone and said, "Hi."

It was Greg from the real estate office.

"Greg, I can't talk now. Bye." She hung up on him and put on her pink cat-eye glasses so she could read the cell phone screen. As she nudged them up higher on her button nose, her cell phone rang again and she jumped, knocking her reading glasses askew; but she could read Joe's name.

Her voice rose and fell as she said, "Hel-lo," sounding like a little girl.

Joe teased her in a southern drawl, "May I speak with your mother, please?" The smooth, slow sound of his voice was like real maple syrup dripping down a stack of pancakes. Joanne's heart did a somersault.

"No, you can't talk with my mother, she died. But you can talk with me if you like." She giggled.

"So, Joanne, how did your day go?"

"Wicked busy. How 'bout yours?"

"Didn't stop all day. Caught a meeting at five o'clock."

"Right. I wanted to go, but the afternoon open house didn't get over until late. How was it?"

"Great! You know somethin'? No matter how shitty I feel before a meeting, I always feel better after it."

"Yeah, I know what you mean."

"Joanne, I have something I really want to tell you."

"Go ahead."

"I'm afraid—"

"Afraid of what?"

"You might go ballistic on me."

"Joe, I wouldn't do that." She heard him take a deep inhale and then let it out.

"Tonight, I agreed to be Zack's sponsor."

"You what?"

"I know helping him is going to help me."

"How can you say that? He is a black-hearted person!"

"Joanne, you don't even know him."

"And I don't want to. I know he never even said he was sorry for the trouble he caused. And I know he is a self-absorbed user. And you just agreed to let him use you."

"Hold on—"

"No, Joe. You hold on. He has zero regard for you."

"Joanne, here's the thing. Please don't interrupt. I used to be just like him. When I met Kitty, I was a total loser. Want to know how we met? I was robbing her home. Yup, she caught me red-handed and didn't turn me in. Want to know why? She had mercy on me. She gave me mercy instead of the punishment I deserved. Didn't someone ever give you a chance? Didn't someone have mercy on you?"

"Yes, but—"

"No buts. Now it's my turn to help someone out. I don't want to die before I can make a difference in someone's life."

"Well, there are lots of people who can use your help. Why him?"

"I just told you. He reminds me of myself when I his age."

"Well, it's your life. I'm just telling you. You give him an inch and he will take a mile. He'll be looking for money or a job or a place to stay. Believe me, I can spot a con artist. All con artists are professional story tellers. Don't get emotionally engaged in his lies."

"I hear you, but you—"

"Like you just said: no buts!"

"No, Joanne. Hear me out. When Kitty caught me stealing from her, she gave me money, a job, and a place to sleep. In time, she gave me her heart. We had forty years of happiness because she gave me mercy from the start."

"That's a beautiful story, but that doesn't mean the same happy ending will happen with Zack."

"Do you know why Kitty gave me mercy?"

"Why? 'Cause you're so handsome?"

Joe chuckled. "No. Well, maybe. But someone gave her mercy, and she wanted to give it too."

"She must have been an amazing person."

"Yeah, she always looked for the good in people and for ways to help the hurting. She gave second chances to people who hurt her because she knew they were hurting. She used to pray to be merciful, and she did acts of mercy every day."

"Maybe I could start by giving Zack the benefit of the

doubt. Next time I see him, I will try not to give him a deadly glare or a snarky retort."

"Good. Because your glances can definitely crush, and your sarcasm is merciless."

Joanne pointed to herself and said, "Me?"

"Seriously, the word sarcasm is derived from the Greek *sarkazein* meaning 'to strip off the flesh.'"

"Ugh!" Joanne said with a grimace.

"Joanne, if you want to practice being merciful, start with yourself. I don't know you that well, but I have heard you cut yourself down a few times."

"Yes, you're right. I have to stop the self-deprecating humor."

"Just the other day I heard you say, 'I'm so stupid,' when you lost your keys. You are not stupid. In fact, your mind is very quick. Next time, instead of beating yourself up, show some mercy on yourself. Notice when you get all cheesed up and take steps to calm down, like pause and breathe. If I lost my keys, you wouldn't say, 'Joe, you're so stupid.' Part of your new beginning could be talking to yourself like you would talk to a friend."

"I'll try."

"When I hear the word mercy, I imagine Jesus as he was dying on the cross. He prayed, 'Father, forgive them for they do not know what they are doing.' That's mercy! Even in his agony, Jesus asked for mercy for his tormentors."

"It's not easy," Joanne said.

"Jesus never promised it would be easy. In fact, practicing mercy takes practice. A lot of practice. Ask the Holy Spirit to help you. Any time you do what is right when you don't feel like it, you grow spiritually."

Joanne took a sip of her water, hopped off the chair, and

walked around, holding her phone. She started coughing. "I have something caught in my throat."

"Is there something you are afraid to say?"

"All this mercy talk makes me uncomfortable."

"Why?"

"Because there are a few people from my past who I still resent. I can't imagine having mercy on them." Then she began to cough again. After she sipped some water, she said, "Joe, I have to go to the bathroom."

"Take your time. I'm goin' nowhere."

Joanne looked into her eyes in the bathroom mirror. *How can I tell him, he will think I'm a loser.* She took a deep inhale and let it out. *Dear God, please give me the courage to be honest with Joe.*

When she returned to her chair and picked up the phone, she hunkered down into its cushions. "Joe, I'm ready. Want to hear a story?"

John was her first love. They were inseparable high school sweethearts. Coming from dysfunctional families, they both wanted to escape. When Joanne discovered she was pregnant, they eloped on her sixteenth birthday. Early in her pregnancy she had a miscarriage. Joanne was devastated, yet she was determined to start a family; but she was never able to conceive again.

John was her life, and she believed their love would last forever. For twenty years it did endure. One morning, as John was going out the door, he turned to her and said, "I won't be coming home tonight. I'm in love with someone and want to marry him."

"Him?" Joanne's life shattered before her. She could not forgive him. All day she would devise ways to kill him. Drinking from morning till night became her way of escaping the pain, until one night in a drunken stupor she slit her wrists. John found her in the bathtub covered in blood and called 911.

When she was able to leave the hospital, he had her admitted to an alcohol treatment center. He then sold their home and moved her into a small condo. Returning to her new home after treatment, she seemed like a new person, and attending AA meetings while studying for her real estate license kept her busy. No one perceived the demons she wrestled with.

One night, a tall, dark, and handsome man whom she immediately recognized sauntered into an AA meeting. He had been at the treatment center with her, and she would never forget his chiseled features or his gift of gab. Wearing an off-white, cable-knit Irish-wool sweater and a patchwork cap, he looked like he just stepped off the boat from Ireland. With his thick, blue-black curly hair and porcelain white skin, he could be mistaken for a model.

He spotted Joanne and gave her a nonchalant wave. She was drawn to his intoxicating blue eyes like a moth to a flame. He walked up to her and said, "Hey, it's me, Liam, remember?"

She bit her lip as a shock of electricity surged through her body. Liam pulled her into him and gave her a strong hug. The coarse wool sweater scratched her face and she flinched. When he stood back and looked into her hungry eyes, his blue eyes twinkled. Joanne was turned on, and he needed a place to sleep. One night led to another and another, and before she knew it, he'd weaseled his way into her life.

AA discourages any kind of romantic involvement in the early stages of sobriety, but Joanne was so hungry for love she didn't care about the rules. With his Irish brogue, Liam could talk her into anything. He possessed a power over her—he knew her vulnerability, and he had every reason you could imagine as to why he didn't have a job.

Before she finally kicked him out, he'd racked up twenty thousand dollars in credit card debt. She hated him for using her, but she hated herself more for falling for his blarney. Because she perceived herself to be a loser, she kept attracting more losers and users into her life.

After she received her real estate license, she decided to turn over a new leaf, and then Mr. Wright breezed into her life. He popped into her first open house. When he introduced himself, he took off his designer sunglasses and dropped them casually on the kitchen counter. Everything about this man was perfect, from his pearly white teeth down to his classic, finely tailored leather loafers. He told her his name was Mason Wright, and he was looking for a home for his mother.

With a killer sense of style, he appeared distinguished and dignified, making Joanne wonder if he had a personal shopper dress him. He was a Dapper Dan. His salt and pepper sideburns gave him an air of sophistication, yet he had an exciting edge and energy about him that caused Joanne to hang on his every word as he chatted about all the places he had traveled. Soon she found herself fantasizing about traveling with him. Little did she know, he was wondering how long it would take for him to access her bank account. Within a week, he had swept her off her feet and moved into her condo with her. Everything seemed to be going well as Joanne began to sell homes and earn some significant cash. Mason began talking to her about the need to invest her funds so the money would begin to work for her instead of sitting in the bank. She trusted him. What she didn't know was that he was a convicted felon on parole and couldn't even land a job.

Joanne told everyone that Mason Wright was the one; they were going to get married. But after about six months,

Mr. Wright became Dr. Jekyll and Mr. Hyde. Mr. Wright's cocktails with dinner turned into cocktails after dinner and throughout most of the night. When she came home from work, he would be there, cocktail in hand, waiting to push her buttons and start the drama. She began drinking again. In their drunken state, they would fight like cats and dogs; and after each bout of name calling and dish throwing, they would make up, and there would be an interim of peace. This went on for months. One night, Mason didn't stop at the name calling and beat Joanne so badly she was left with a black eye, three cracked ribs, and a chip in her left front tooth. The volatile relationship ended abruptly the night Joanne overdosed on pills and alcohol, landing her in the hospital for a month and back into rehab.

In the meantime, her ex-husband and his partner had a chat with Mr. Wright, and when Joanne returned home, the condo showed no trace of his ever being there. Even the scent of his irresistible cologne was missing from the air. The only thing remaining was her empty bank account and thirty thousand dollars of debt in her name.

Joanne sold her condo but was unable to make a significant dent in the debt she had been saddled with, let alone pay for two stays in rehab. Next, she sold anything she had of value, including all her expensive furniture, gold jewelry, designer clothes, shoes, and Italian leather bags—everything she believed defined her—but still was unable to pay all she owed.

"So, Joe. Sometimes I wonder how I could have been so stupid."

"Joanne, please stop calling yourself stupid. Next time you do, stop and say something good about yourself instead."

"Well, what's your opinion of me, now that you know the truth?"

"You know, it's not what I think that matters. In Matthew 5:44, Jesus said, 'Love your enemies and pray for those who persecute you.' The words in that verse is what Christianity is all about. You can't call yourself a Christian if you have hate in your heart, plus it's bad for your health."

"Yes, Joe, but—"

"No buts! Those predators hurt you, I understand. And here is the 'but': No one can hurt you unless you allow them to hurt you."

"Yeah. I heard a quote by Eleanor Roosevelt that says, 'No one can make you feel inferior without your permission.'"

"The important thing to remember is not to judge yourself."

"Yes, I am going to practice, practice, practice!"

"Hate is a mighty powerful emotion. It's like a poisonous venom that pollutes your soul. Do you want to do that to your beautiful soul?"

"Of course not."

"Well, at the very heart of hate is blame and that's where your pain is. Deep down you blame yourself and try to punish yourself. Take, for instance, your compulsion for sugar. That was a form of self-hatred manifesting itself."

"Yes, I know."

"It's easy to have mercy on someone you love, right? Well, why can't you have mercy on yourself? Do you not love yourself?"

"Um, no," she said.

"Jesus taught us to have mercy on everyone. All the trials you have been through have all been lessons. And all those men were your teachers. God orchestrated every single detail to bring you to this very moment today. Can you imagine that? If it weren't for John and Liam and Mr. Wright, I wouldn't even know you. I'd like to thank those guys right after I punch them out." He chuckled.

"I've never stopped to consider it like that. You are so right. When you think of how flawed we all are, I wanted something from each of them as much as they wanted something from me." Joanne paused for a moment. "I choose to have mercy on them and myself."

"Joanne, the first step is awareness. Write yourself a letter about all the hate you feel. Just let it rip. Get it all out of your head and heart. Remember, in Matthew 9:13, Jesus said, 'Blessed are the merciful, for they shall receive mercy.'"

"Thanks, Joe. I feel better already. I'm looking forward to seeing you tomorrow night."

REFLECTION

Examine your heart today. Is there anyone in your life who needs your mercy? Why not give it to them? It's the right thing to do. Choose mercy!

Remember, the one who hurts you is hurting themselves more.

It's hard to be merciful if you're without humility. Pray for both.

ACTION TIP

This week try to do one act of mercy every day.

Surrender to God and choose to show mercy before you get out of bed in the morning.

You can make a difference. Go to YouTube and view the "Divine Mercy Chaplet Prayer." Take time to pray for the whole world.

PETITION

Dear God,

Thank You for Your mercy. Please send the Holy Spirit to help me develop an attitude of mercy. Thank You for sending Jesus to show us how to be merciful. Please open my heart to receive Your gift of mercy so I can be merciful to myself and the world.

CHAPTER 8

Anticipation

Joe met his clients at the construction site of their home to discuss ideas, style, and budget for the new landscape. Filled with nervous anticipation about his first date in forty years, he couldn't concentrate on the conversation about the plans. He cut the meeting short, jumped in his truck, and took off to the mall.

Joe strode into the jewelry store like a man on a mission. As he surveyed the jewelry case, a 14-karat gold, heart-shaped, aquamarine pendant captured his attention. Tiny, glittering diamonds circled and harmonized with the blue stone.

"Perfect!"

While he waited to have it wrapped, he checked his messages. His next appointment canceled, and he uttered a soft, "Thank You, God." Now he had the afternoon free to get ready.

On his way out of the mall, Joe passed a men's store with a mannequin dressed in an aquamarine, plaid madras shirt in the window. *I really like that color.* Entering the store, he found a salesperson and asked, "Is that shirt in the window for sale?"

"Yes, but it's the last one."

"Great! I'll take it."

"What about the size?"

"Oh, it's my size."

With the most important goals accomplished, he strutted to his truck like a proud peacock.

Next, he dropped his truck off at the express auto detailing shop. While it was being washed, waxed, polished, and deodorized, he went to the barber shop next door and had his hair washed, cut, and styled. The barber trimmed his bushy eyebrows and mustache. As the barber was finishing, Joe asked, "Can you do my nose, too?"

"Joe! Got a hot date tonight?"

"Yup!" Joe said with a gleam in his eyes.

"Good for you. Hope you have a fun time."

"Thanks," Joe replied, and his face lit up as he looked in the mirror. *Not bad for an old fart.*

Joanne's morning was jam packed, but she cleared time in the afternoon for a gel manicure and a pedicure.

Strolling into the salon, the receptionist greeted her with "Pick a color."

Joanne glanced over at the rack of nail polish even though she had already decided on La Paz-itively Hot Pink. She positioned herself comfortably in the electric massage chair while the technician set the timer and began the massage. Once her feet dipped into the warm water, her stress melted away, it was like a mini jacuzzi. Small jets pulsated water against the tired soles of her feet. She closed her eyes and started daydreaming about Joe. For the first time, it occurred to her that she had never kissed a man with a mustache. When the technician began to massage her legs, Joanne looked down. *Look at the hair on those legs. Why didn't I shave this morning?* Looking at her legs brought her attention back to Joe's mustache. *What if it tickles or makes me sneeze?*

Staring at the technician, Joanne raised a quizzical eyebrow, *I wonder if she would know how it feels to kiss a guy with a mustache.*

"Excuse me, I didn't catch your name."

"Anna." The technician smiled.

"Anna, do you know anything about mustaches?"

"Yes, we wax for you today."

"Uh … no, thank you." Undeterred, Joanne grabbed her phone and googled "What does it feel like to kiss a guy with a mustache." Scrolling through she couldn't find any positive feedback. One gal said, "… hair got stuck in my teeth and in my throat." *Yuck!* Another lady said, "… it was like kissing a pin cushion." But the best quote was "… it shouldn't be asking too much to go through a briar patch to get to a picnic." All at once she did a double take at the word mustache—must ache! Joanne threw her phone into her bag, pressed the button to recline the chair, and let out a huge exhale. *Okay, the what-if thinking must stop now.*

While Anna massaged Joanne's legs with hot stones, the prickly thoughts disappeared. Soon she drifted into a state of tranquility.

The first thing Joanne did when she returned home was turn on the water for a shower. After she got the temperature exactly right, she stripped down and stepped in, humming a song. Even though she couldn't carry a tune, she still believed she sounded rather good in the shower. When she finished shaving her legs, she used the razor as her microphone and belted out a song as her feelings of anxiousness washed down the drain. She followed up her vocal stylings by performing a pole dance using the grab bar as she stepped carefully out of the shower, and she continued dancing with uninhibited glee as she dried off. The show was dramatically cut short, however, when she danced off the fluffy bathmat, slipped, and fell on her butt. Joanne rubbed her bum and winced. *Thank God I have a lot of padding.* She tried to see if she had bruised, but the good thing about her bathroom mirror was it only reflected from the waist up and she never had to look at her dimpled derriere.

After she moisturized her body, she stepped into her big-girl, butt-lifting panty. Next, she put on her add-a-size bra. Just as she was bending over to get her boobs in place in her new bra, the phone rang. *Oh no! I hope it's not Joe canceling our date.* When she squinted at the screen, she didn't recognize the number, and she let out a sigh of relief before she answered. It was a new client hoping to schedule a coaching session on Monday at five o'clock. The woman talked on and on about her problem. Finally able to get off the phone, Joanne scurried to finish getting ready. As she pulled her golden spiral curls up into a ponytail, she gasped. *I forgot to shave my armpits!* She looked at the clock. *Another delay.*

She applied tinted moisturizer to her face and noticed her hands were shaky. The first date jitters were freaking her out. Immediately, she stopped everything and did some breathing exercises. Out loud, she repeated, "I have plenty of time." In no time at all, she was calm and able to outline her lips with a lip pencil. Then she filled them in with her long-lasting, hot-pink lipstick. After she swiped a bit of lip gloss on her bottom lip, she smacked her lips together and said, "Luscious."

Next, she stepped into her blue and white shirtwaist dress with a stand-up collar and a coordinated sash that cinched her waist. Leaving the top two buttons open, she dabbed perfume on her décolletage.

Walking out of the room, she pulled her stomach in and

threw her shoulders back, and glancing in the mirror, batted her eyelashes. *Thank God for eyelash extensions.*

At that moment, Joanne heard a loud knock. Opening the door, she stopped and stared at Joe. For the first time in all her fifty-six years on earth, Joanne was speechless. In that space of nothingness, something happened deep inside her; it was more than physical excitement. It was sheer bliss.

Finally, in a high-pitched, squeaky voice she said, "Oh! Come in, come in. How silly of me to leave you standing there."

Joe's mustache trembled, and his heart did a flip-flop. His fingers were curled tight around a small box wrapped in gold paper and tied with a blue ribbon. *It might take a crowbar to pry my fingers loose.* When Joe stepped forward, he stumbled over the threshold, and the box popped out of his hands. Joanne caught it by surprise, and they both started laughing.

Joe stared at Joanne as she unwrapped the gift. "I'm going to save this ribbon. In fact, I'll wear it in my hair tonight," she said.

When she opened the box, she said, "It's gorgeous! How did you know my birthstone?"

"Um, actually, I didn't. When I saw it, I liked the way it sparkled and shined, just like you."

"Thank you, Joe." Joanne looked into his eyes. "No one has ever given me such a thoughtful gift. I will cherish it forever. Could you please hook it on me?" Joanne turned her collar down and Joe stood behind her. As his clumsy fingers fumbled with the clasp, she could feel his warm breath on her neck. Finishing, he placed both his hands gently on her shoulders and kissed the back of her neck. The silky softness of his mustache on her skin sent a tingly sensation through her body. Abruptly, she pulled away and ran into the bathroom on the pretense that she wanted to look at the pendant in the mirror. She leaned on the sink to hold herself up, she was so weak in the knees. Then she looked in the mirror. *You can't wait any longer. You have to tell him tonight.*

They sat under an umbrella at a table overlooking the harbor. It was a perfect night to eat outside. They both decided on hot boiled lobsters. For starters, Joe ordered a cup of clam chowder.

Joe inhaled the salt air as he sprinkled the tiny crackers on his chowder. Joanne closed her eyes and listened to the sound of the sea gulls and the clanking of the halyards against the masts on the sailboats. It was like a private concert of wind chimes.

"Lobster is a messy meal," the waiter said as he gave them bibs and extra napkins.

"Did you know back in the old days, lobster was nicknamed 'cockroach of the sea'; it was a poor man's protein," Joe said.

"Speaking of the little devils, here they come."

"Nothing little about these guys. Do you want me to help you crack yours open?"

"No thanks, that's the fun of it!" Joanne cracked the hard shell, and it flew across the table. Joe ducked.

"Good thing you have on your bib. Maybe I need to get a shield," Joe said. She picked out a huge chunk of lobster meat and dunked it into the sweet drawn butter.

"Scrumptious." Joanne's eyes twinkled. "Thank you, Joe."

With melted butter dripping down her chin, Joanne had a sweaty, disheveled look. Joe held his hand over his mouth to cover a smile, but when Joanne broke off the lobster's little legs and started sucking on them to get the tiny morsels of tender meat, he doubled over laughing.

"Sorry, it looked like you were eating the shells." Pulling out his cell, he leaned in and snapped a picture. "I don't want to forget this moment," he said as he reached across the table to brush a lobster crumb out of her hair.

Joanne flinched. A fleeting smile crossed her face as she shook her head and said, "I'm a hot mess!"

Joe burst into a loud guffaw. "You're hot, alright!"

She gave him a coy look and her smile came back. Joanne's voice went down an octave. "Thanks, I think." She turned her head to avert his eyes, but her blush gave her away.

After the waiter cleared the table, he came back with hot towels and finger bowls filled with warm water; slices of lemon floated on top. While Joanne gently dipped each of her fingers in the warm water, she cleared her throat. Looking down at the bowl of water, unable to meet Joe's eyes, she said, "There is something I have to tell you right now." She reached across and took his hand out of his finger bowl, placing it in hers. As she rubbed each of his fingers, Joe held his breath and his eyes glassed over. Then she whispered, "It's tempting to swish and play in the water."

"Uh-huh."

She stroked his fingers and said, "Well, that's what I want to talk about."

In his throaty voice, he said, "You want to talk about playing in the water?"

"No, silly. I'm talking about temptation."

REFLECTION

When was the last time you anticipated something? Sometimes looking forward to something is even more pleasurable than the pleasure itself. The nice thing about looking forward to something is it doesn't cost anything.

ACTION TIP

Every day this week make an intention to anticipate something wonderful. Find the joy in the anticipation. Things to anticipate: a new book, a new show on TV, a new hobby, or a new craft. Perhaps watching a sunset or a sunrise. Maybe learning how to meditate or trying your hand at art.

Think about ways to anticipate more fun. Watch how it lifts your spirit. Perk yourself up and get out of your rut.

PETITION

Dear God,

I anticipate a deeper relationship with You. Help me to learn how to delay gratification and learn how to wait for Your timing.

CHAPTER 9

Chastity

oe shot her a double take. "Did you say temptation?"

"Uh-huh, you are tempting to me." Joanne blushed, let go of his hand, and cast her eyes down. "I want to jump in and play with you, but I can't." Her face turned as red as the lobster.

Joe's mouth fell open and his eyes blinked. Fidgeting with a spoon on the table, Joanne said, "Ten years ago … ten years ago right now, in fact, I decided to be chaste."

Joe was speechless. She watched his Adam's apple go up and down. *He must think I'm a religious fanatic.* Desperately, she searched his face, waiting.

"Chaste?" he finally said.

"Yeah," she said as she wrung her hands under the table.

"You'll never know how relieved I am to hear that."

Joanne gave him a quizzical look. "Relieved?"

"You bet!" He rubbed his forehead. "I've, um, been struggling to find the words to tell you—"

Joanne's heart sank. "Tell me what?"

"I was afraid to tell you—"

"Tell me what?" Joanne's voice changed pitch.

"I was afraid you'd think I was a weirdo."

"What is it?" she yelled, causing other patrons to turn in their seats.

Joe glanced out at the boats in the harbor. Then he closed his eyes and leaned back in his chair. She watched his chest expand as his lungs filled up with air. When he exhaled, a smile spread across his face.

"I believe sex outside of marriage separates us from God," he said.

Joanne looked at Joe incredulously. "Me too," she squealed.

"What made you decide to be chaste?"

"I had a spiritual encounter."

"Really?" Joe's eyes widened. "What happened?" he asked as he balanced on the edge of his chair.

"Well, let me take you back to that day."

Joanne leaned back in her seat and formed a steeple with her fingers. Her face was lit up and animated as she described the sultry day that changed her life forever.

It was the first day of the women's silent retreat, and it was unusually hot. At one o'clock, Joanne was scheduled to go on a walking meditation. Outside, the humidity wrapped around her like a bathrobe. Even the flowers were wilting. Instead, she ducked into the air-conditioned chapel.

During a quiet moment of Eucharistic adoration, something happened.

An ornate gold monstrance with a large sunburst design was on the altar. In it, behind a small round glass, she could see the Eucharist. Kneeling there, in the presence of the Body of Christ, filled her with a sense of awe. She breathed in the lingering scent of incense and whispered, "Here I am, Lord."

Fascinated by the flickering flames of the candles on the

alter, she relaxed. Slowly she closed her eyes. She opened them slightly and was surprised by dazzling white light beams coming from the sunburst on the monstrance. The light radiated through her. She knew the light was love. God was filling her with His unconditional love. She had searched for so long to find a way to fill that empty space, but nothing could satisfy her hunger until now. And now the search was over.

She opened her eyes wide, and the light became dissipated, but she still felt the heat in her chest and her quickening heartbeat. Even though it was only a split second, something did happen, and Joanne knew her life might never be the same.

Silent tears of joy welled up in her eyes. Spellbound, she sat on the cool hard bench and sensed the sacredness. The smooth oak wood of the pew had a clean scent of Murphy Oil Soap. *I want my soul to be clean.*

On the bench next to her was a copy of St. Augustine's *Confessions*. Picking it up, it opened to the first page, and in yellow marker someone had underlined the words, "For Thou hast made us for Thyself and our hearts are restless till they rest in Thee." The words resonated deep within Joanne's heart, and she understood all her inner emptiness was a gift from God to bring her to Him and to His love.

Joanne was talking so fast she couldn't catch her breath. She took a sip of water and hugged herself.

"Are you cold?" Joe asked.

"No, no, let me finish. Where was I? Oh! I know."

Right then and there Joanne decided to make her relationship with God her top priority in life. She desired to glorify Him and honor Him with her body. She knew she wanted to be chaste.

"Wow! Let's drink to chastity." They clinked their glasses and said in unison, "To chastity!"

Joanne continued. "God surprised me."

"How?"

She bounced in her seat and in a bubbly voice said, "He took away my sexual obsession. For the past ten years, I have not been tempted to be unchaste."

Joe gave her a slow smile, feeling his tension release.

Joanne said, "You know, something else happened in that chapel. Jesus placed a mission in my heart. I knew He was calling me to help other people with addictions and teach about His transforming love."

"There are so many people suffering from soul-sickness in our world," said Joe.

Joanne had a radiant glow. Her eyes crinkled at the corners as she explained her plan. "Someday, I hope to open a retreat center for healing, but until then, I am grateful for my coaching business and—Hey, Joe! Look down there on the dock!" Joanne pointed. "Isn't that Zack?"

Immediately Joe saw the passion in Joanne's eyes disappear. Her eyes narrowed and her nostrils flared.

"Yeah, it's Zack. I hired him to help me with my boat."

"Boat?"

"Yeah. That's what I wanted to show you after dinner." Joe jerked to his feet, nearly tipping his chair over. "I'll be right back. I'm going to the truck to get some sweatshirts."

Joanne didn't say a word. Instead, she glared at Zack. As soon as Joe was out of sight, she muttered to herself, "That little weasel." In that instant, Joe's words about mercy came back to her. She tipped her head back and closed her eyes. *God, please give me the grace to see You in Zack.*

While Joe was walking back to his truck, he texted Zack, "Is everything shipshape?"

"Yes, I just put a few cold drinks in the fridge."

"Okay, get going."

"Aye aye, captain."

When Joe came back, he handed Joanne a light-blue chambray hoodie. Printed on the back, in bold white letters, was "Serenity."

"Here, you might want to put this on. There's a cool breeze off the water tonight."

As she pulled it on over her head, she sniffed a heavenly scent of laundry detergent and a hint of sandalwood. It felt so light and soft against her skin.

"Looking good. You are now an official crew member of the *Serenity*."

Joanne laid her hand on his back, and when he turned around, she gave him a hug. "Thank you, so much," she whispered in his ear.

He took her hand and led her down the ramp to the dock.

Joanne slipped her sandals off and climbed aboard the thirty-five-foot Catalina sailboat. After he gave her a tour of the roomy galley down below, they stretched out on top in the comfortable cockpit.

"Lounging on these soft cushions and listening to the soothing sound of the lapping water is seventh heaven."

With a gleam in his eyes, Joe said, "Know what would be better?"

Joanne tilted her head to the side and fluttered her lashes. "What?"

"A sunset cruise on Buzzards Bay."

"Really?"

"Yup!"

"My first sailboat ride!"

After Joe started the engine, they quietly motored out of

the harbor. As they came about to hoist the sail, Joe said, "Can you take the helm?"

Joanne gripped the wheel so tight that her knuckles turned white.

Joe yelled, "Just keep it pointed into the wind."

After Joe raised the sail, he shut off the engine and they were sailing. Feeling the wind in her face as they carved a path through the sea was the most exhilarating experience of her life.

As the boat gently heeled in the breeze, she watched the spectacular sunset, and Joe watched her with a yearning in his heart. Basking in the afterglow of the sunset, Joanne felt connected to God.

"Look at these waves." Joe pointed. "They're getting bigger and bigger. But don't worry, eventually they'll die down. We just have to ride 'em out. Like temptation gets stronger and stronger, but if we ride it out, it will weaken and subside." Joe put his arm around her shoulder and said, "Joanne, we can ride anything out together with the grace of God."

She leaned into him and looked into his eyes. "That reminds me of the scripture from Matthew 19:26, 'With God, all things are possible.'"

"Right. We have to remember that. Sometimes we can be our own worst enemy."

"Tell me about it," Joanne said, rolling her eyes.

Joe tapped his thumb against the wheel and kept his arm around Joanne. He smiled. "Talking about temptation, can I tempt you to a sleepover tonight?"

"Sleepover? Tonight, on the boat?"

"There's nothing better than sleeping on a boat. It's like rocking in a cradle."

"But I'm not prepared."

"Who cares? The boat is ready. What do you need?"

"Well, a toothbrush would be nice," she huffed and crossed her arms.

"There's one in the head. New, just for you."

"Well," she said, turning away. Dazzled by the beauty of the glistening black water in the light of the waning crescent moon, Joanne couldn't concentrate. Her thoughts tossed about like the waves. *It is tempting, but I don't have any clean underwear for tomorrow.*

Joe placed a hand on his chest. The way he said "Please" sent a warm wave through her.

"Take the wheel. We're heading in." Then he pulled out his phone and called Zack. "We're on our way back. Thanks." Turning to Joanne he said, "When we get in, Zack will be there to help with the lines and dock the boat. He'll give you some lessons so you'll know what to do next time. Now relax and enjoy the ride."

She sprawled on the long cushion. As she gazed out at the water, she twirled a loose curl around her finger.

"Why the worried look?"

"Hmm. I'm not worried, just thinking."

"'Bout what?"

"I'd love to sleepover, but I wish I had planned."

"If you planned, it wouldn't be an adventure. Spontaneity is more fun."

"Ooh, I like the sound of that."

She turned around and gave Joe a big grin, "Count me in!"

"Woo-hoo!" Joe slapped the wheel. Then he turned on the running lights, and they motored into the harbor. At first there was an eerie stillness as they carefully crept along, but as they got closer to the dock, the sound of music broke the silence.

"Where's the music coming from?"

Joe pointed toward the restaurant. "Up there. There's dancing under the stars."

"Dancing?"

"Yeah. Do you like to dance?"

"I love to! I haven't been out dancing since my cousin Jimmy's wedding. It must have been five years ago."

"Well, we'll have to fix that tonight!"

Joanne laughed and leaned back. She clasped her hands behind her head and said, "You maneuver this boat so well."

"Thanks. I can't wait to maneuver you on the dance floor."

Joanne let out a loud "Mwah-ha-ha! Speaking of maneuvering, there's Zack on the dock."

"Now be nice. That guy is a godsend."

Joanne frowned and sat up. "A godsend?"

"Yup! He spent all day getting the boat ready so we could go sailing tonight. Boats get dirty and smelly."

Joanne looked down and said, "I'll try to be nice, but I'm not making any promises."

REFLECTION

Nearly every religion teaches the principle of chastity before marriage, but fewer people are observing it. It is one of the seven virtues. Why does our society no longer value chastity?

ACTION TIP

Don't rely on just yourself to stay chaste. Ask God for strength in a tempting situation. Remember it will pass.

Practice self-mastery. Once you change your perspective, everything changes.

It is impossible to ignore that Jesus said sex outside of marriage separates us from Him. It doesn't matter if you are sixteen or eighty-six. The separation from God causes soul-sickness no matter how old you are.

PETITION

Dear God,

I want to deepen my relationship with You. Please bless me with the grace to live a holy and pleasing life.

CHAPTER 10

Humility

oe swung his arm out and gestured toward Zack. "That guy is a seasoned sailor."

Joanne lifted an eyebrow. "Oh, really?"

"Yes," Joe said. "Really."

She curled her lip and shook her head. "How do you know that?"

"He told me."

"He told you," she repeated. "And you believed him?" Grabbing Joe by his shoulders Joanne's voice rose. "Don't you see it?"

"See what?"

Joanne threw her hands into the air. "Zack lies like a bragging sailor. He's full of fish tales!"

"No, no, Joanne," Joe said, wagging his finger at her. "Zack isn't bragging. I did some digging and his story checked out. He grew up boating on Miami's Biscayne Bay. It was there he learned about sailing and boat maintenance."

"Yes, and drug dealing!"

Joe muttered, "Please." They stared at each other for a long moment. Finally, Joe opened his mouth to speak but Joanne put up her hand. He flinched.

"Joe, I don't want to see anyone take advantage of your kindness."

Joe blew out a noisy breath. "Joanne, please don't make the disrespectful mistake of assuming you know Zack before you take the time to learn the truth about him."

Joanne pulled the hood of the sweatshirt up to cover her head, and she stuffed her hands into the pockets. She turned away from Joe. *Mistake? As soon as I get off this boat, I'm calling an Uber to take me home.*

After Joe docked the boat he said to Joanne, "Throw Zack that blue line."

Tossing the line to Zack, she noticed the moonlight softened the hard angles of his face. *He looks different tonight.*

Zack tied the line and turned to Joanne. "Thanks. Now may I take your purse and shoes?"

She gave him a blank stare as she handed them to him.

"It's important to have your hands free when you disembark a boat," Zack said. He placed her things on a nearby bench and came back to help her. Reaching out his hand, he said, "Grab my wrist. That's more secure."

A shudder went through Joanne as she stepped onto the dock. Quickly she slipped into her sandals and waved. "Bye, guys."

"Hey!" Joe hollered, "Where are you going?" When she didn't answer, he went after her. "Joanne! Wait!" he said, grabbing her hand.

Joanne clutched her purse with her other hand and said, "I have to go."

"But what about the sleepover?" Then he pulled her close.

"I changed my mind," she said, jerking away from him.

"Jo, please stay," Joe pleaded. He pushed her hood back away from her face. They closed their eyes. He leaned into her. Her heart skipped a beat as his silky mustache covered her lips and his kiss stole her breath. When he pulled her closer, she inhaled sharply as she tried to pull away. Joe studied her face looking for answers.

"I don't like you criticizing me." Joanne blubbered like a child.

"I'm sorry I hurt your feelings. Please forgive me." His hands found their way to the sides of her wet face, and he kissed her tears away. Stinging tears filled her eyes.

Joe took her hand and led her onto the dance floor. While he held her in his arms, she rested her head on his chest. Listening to the rhythm of his heartbeat in sync with hers made her feel completely connected to him. Under the stars they swayed to the music, and as they danced the night away, they reached new heights of happiness.

In silence, they walked hand in hand back to the boat. Joe drew Joanne close one more time and whispered in her ear, "Thank you for making me feel alive again."

As soon as Joanne lay her head down on the fluffy down pillow and pulled the puffy duvet close to her chin, she was overwhelmed with gratitude and she prayed, *I am grateful for the beautiful pendant, the delicious lobster dinner, the wonderful sail, the gorgeous sunset, the fun dancing, the music, being with Joe, and for his sweet kiss. Dear God, thank You for the best day of my life, and please bless Joe.*

With a start she realized she nearly missed out on this wonderful night. *Why do I have to behave like such a spoiled brat? Talk about missing the boat!* She wrestled with her guilty conscience about her resentment of Zack. Turning at last to

God she said softly, "Please help me. Please give me a humble spirit. Let me know my absurdity before I act absurdly. And God, please help Zack."

When Joanne finally drifted off to sleep, she slept like a baby. As dawn broke, she stirred to the smell of coffee and the murmured voice of Joe up in the cockpit. She climbed the ladder and popped her head out. "Morning, Joe!"

Joe raised his coffee mug and smiled. "Hey, Miss Sunshine! Want a cup?"

"I'd love one, thanks. Black, please," she said as she came out onto the deck.

"Sit here. You don't want to miss this show."

"Show?"

Joe stretched out his arms and said, "The sunrise!"

"Ooh! I will treasure this moment with you forever. Thank You, Lord," she said aloud.

"Look, the sun is coming up. Isn't it amazing?"

"Yes, it is. And today I get double the pleasure to see all the colors of the sunrise reflected on the water. Gives me goosebumps!"

"Look at all those shades of red. That red sky is giving you a rosy glow, Jo."

She stretched her hands out and spread her fingers like a star fish to see pink reflected on her hands. Breathing in the poignant air she asked, "Have you heard the old adage, 'Red sky at night, sailor's delight; red sky in the morning, sailors take warning'?"

"Sure."

"Well, is it true?"

"Oh, yeah." Joe stretched out his legs and took a sip of coffee. "The concept is over two thousand years old, and it's referenced in the Bible."

"Really?"

"Definitely." Joe ran his fingers through his hair and cleared his throat. "Let me see, how does it go?"

Then he told Joanne about the Pharisees testing Jesus and asking for signs from heaven. One day Jesus answered them with what Matthew recorded in verses 16:2–3: "When it is evening, you say, 'It will be fair weather; for the sky is red.' And in the morning, 'It will be stormy today, for the sky is red and threatening.' You know how to interpret the appearance of the sky, but you cannot interpret the signs of the times."

"Wow!"

"Sounds like Jesus is talking to us. There are signs all around us, but no one is looking at the signs of our times." After a moment he asked, "Joanne, would you meditate with me this morning?"

"I would love to. Every day as the sun rises, it gives us a new beginning," she said. "When you breathe in, breathe in love, and when you breathe out, let go of regret."

"Let's greet today with an open mind and an open heart. This is the perfect place. It feels sacred."

Joanne spoke softly, "Feel the awe of the beautiful colors of the sunrise. Let the light seep in through your gently closed eyelids. Feel the wave of gratitude flow through you and then come back to being aware of your breath. Notice your breath as it goes up your nose and out your nose. Breathe in the love and breathe out the regret. Then let go, be still, and feel God's presence."

"Mmm, it feels good to meditate with you."

"Being with you is beyond blissful." She closed her eyes and tipped her head back.

"It's supposed to start raining late this morning. I was

wondering if we could attend morning mass and go out to breakfast afterward."

"That would be great," Joanne said, "but I have to be home by eleven."

"Are you kidding?"

"No. I have to show a house at noon."

Joe rubbed the back of his neck and muttered, "Damn!"

Joanne stroked his arm. "Sorry, Joe. Some people are only free to look at homes on the weekend."

"No worries." He handed her a fresh cup of coffee.

"Thanks."

"How'd you sleep last night?"

She met his eyes and placed her hands over her heart. "Wonderful, once I finally fell asleep."

"You had trouble?"

"At first. I couldn't stop thinking about how I almost ruined the whole night. And then I had an epiphany."

"An epiphany?" Joe tapped his fingers together. "Tell me about it."

"Well, I, um, perhaps I need to practice a bit more humility myself." She shrugged. "Why does the mere mention of Zack's name drive me insane?"

Joe formed a steeple with his hands and asked, "Have you heard of Marian Keyes?"

Joanne shook her head. "No, I haven't."

"Well, she is an Irish novelist who Kitty always quoted. One quote in particular made an impression on me. 'The things we dislike most in others are the characteristics we like least about ourselves.'"

Joanne took off her sunglasses and wiped her eyes with the sleeve of her sweatshirt. "That is so true." She fidgeted with her pendant. "Last night it occurred to me that Zack obviously stirs up some kind of insecurity in me."

Turning his head slightly, Joe tried to hide a smile. For a moment, there was an awkward pause, but then Joanne continued to babble away.

"Yup. So, I decided next time his arrogance annoys me, I won't talk about him. Instead, I will look within myself at my own faults."

"You know, Jo," he said, "even the smallest act of humility is a step to being closer to God."

A flush crept up her face. "I'm sorry for acting like a spoiled child last night. Please forgive me."

Joe took her chin in one hand and turned her face so that he could look into her blue eyes. "I appreciate your apology, beautiful lady."

"Thank you, Joe. I learned the hard way," she said. "There's nothing more damaging in a relationship than when one person can't admit they were wrong."

Joe squeezed her shoulder. Fumbling for the right words to say, he continued, "Personally, humility was the hardest lesson in my life to learn."

"Joe, you don't have an arrogant bone in your body."

"Oh, but I did. I was always rooted in arrogance. Then God put Kitty in my life. She was the most humble person you could ever meet. Right up there with Mother Teresa. God never gives up teaching us lessons until we learn what we need to know."

"Wow." Joanne's eyes twinkled. "Maybe there's hope for me."

REFLECTION

What were Joanne's insecurities?

Why did Zack annoy her?

She didn't want to be arrogant, but was she?

How about you?

Would your life be different today if you were more humble?

ACTION TIP

Each night ask yourself:

Was I arrogant today?

Did I let pride get in the way?

Did I act snobbish or vain?

Each day:

Make an attempt to listen to others.

Take the time to be present.

Accept what is, without judging.

Count your blessings.

PETITION

Dear God,

Please keep me free from the temptations of pride and arrogance. Please, will You bless me with the gift of humility. Thank You for opening my heart to see the beauty of humility.

CHAPTER 11

Courage

When the truck stopped in front of her apartment, Joanne smiled at Joe.

"I hate to go, but you know I have to."

"Yeah, I do, but I miss you already." Joe slid out of his seat and went around to help her down.

With the warm summer raindrops gently falling on their heads, they kissed. Joe pushed his lips into hers.

"Mmm," she sighed.

After she felt the dopamine rush, Joanne pulled back and focused on his face. Joe leaned in and rested his forehead against hers.

"Thank you," he whispered.

She inhaled his scent and the sweet smell of the summer shower. It stirred something deep inside her. She inhaled again, only this time more deeply. She felt close to swooning. But suddenly the spell was broken like a mirror dropped on a marble floor.

"Hey, Joanne!" her loud-mouthed neighbor screeched. She came running up to them, prepared for the rain in a yellow rain slicker. "Well, well, well. Look what the cat dragged in," Louise said in a raspy voice.

Joanne stiffened. *What a pain in the neck!*

"Louise, this is Joe. Joe, this is my neighbor Louise."

Joe turned to hop into the safety of his truck as he said over his shoulder, "Nice to meet you, Louise." Before she could open her mouth to give him the third degree, he took off like a bat out of hell.

Joanne turned and trotted up the steps. "Gotta run!"

Louise stood outside in the sultry, tropical rain looking up into the sky. *Those clouds look ominous. I hope that guy doesn't have far to drive.*

Gazing straight ahead, Joe drove in a hypnotic state. The rain drumming on the hood of his truck and the monotonous hiss of his tires on the wet highway lulled him into a false sense of security. When he turned the radio on, the squish, squish, squish sound of the windshield wipers kept perfect rhythm with the song that came on, and he sang along.

The steady rain became a deluge as heavy as Joe had ever driven in, and it began to obscure his vision. The truck's wipers were no match for the torrent, and his visibility dropped to zero. Traffic fell to a crawl, and then a standstill turning the highway into a long, narrow parking lot. Flashing lights finally gave notice of an accident up ahead.

Black clouds sprawled across the sky and thunder boomed. Joe shuddered noticing the rain on the roof of the truck sounded like bullets. When a streak of hot, silver lightening lit up the sky, a nameless fear clutched Joe's heart and triggered haunting flashbacks of his time in Vietnam.

A police car raced by with its siren screaming and its lights ablaze. Off in the distance, Joe could hear the wail of an ambulance, but the loud rumble of thunder almost drowned it out. A firetruck came roaring past, and Joe reflexively put his hands over his ears. In that moment, the thunder cracked like a giant whip, and Joe's knee began to bounce up and down. To stop his leg from jiggling, he rubbed his sweaty right hand down the front of his jeans, wiping beads of perspiration from his forehead with his left forearm. He wanted to pray for all the people in the accident, but he was unable to focus. Then he remembered how Joanne guided him in meditation just that morning. He closed his eyes and placed his hands on his thighs with his palms up. Over and over again, he slowly took a breath in and released it out, becoming aware of the sensation of his blood flowing through the veins in his hands. After a few moments, he noticed a tingling in his fingertips. When he gently opened his eyes, he began to appreciate the beauty of the chaos before him, and his heart overflowed with gratitude. He closed his eyes and continued to breathe.

The sudden wash of bliss took him by surprise. He had a sense of being connected and in harmony with the whole universe even as the storm raged all around. A calm surrounded him like a soft blanket and, feeling God's love, he let go of his fear.

The words to a catchy tune he had heard in church wiggled their way into his head, and he couldn't get the sticky song out of his mind. Joe decided to go with the flow of the moment and began singing, humming when he didn't remember the words.

> No storm can shake my inmost calm,
> While to that rock I'm clinging.
> Since Love is Lord of heaven and earth,
> How can I keep from singing?

Eventually, the traffic began to move as did the stormy

weather. Its dark clouds rolled away. Rays of sunshine burst through the misty rain forming a rainbow just ahead of him. Joe was awestruck and called out, "Thank You, Lord!"

The traffic cleared, and as he drove, he began to debate whether he should attend the grief support meeting Joanne had suggested. He turned on the radio and fiddled with the knob. The song "Over the Rainbow" sprang forth from the speakers, startling him. Kitty had chosen that song as the background music for the slideshow commemorating her life, and it had played during the luncheon following her funeral.

Hearing the song seemed to reignite his grief. "Oh, Kitty," and a dam of sorrow burst, releasing warm, pent-up tears. "Kitty, I miss you," Joe whimpered, banging his hand on the steering wheel. His intense reaction to the song convinced Joe he needed to attend the grief support meeting … he needed to find a way to deal with unexpected reminders of Kitty.

When Joe walked into the room, he fought the desire to walk back out. A heaviness settled in the bottom of his stomach leaving him feeling dizzy, and he held on to the back of a nearby chair to steady himself.

"You okay?" asked a pretty woman who walked in behind him.

"Yes, yes, I am." He slowly lowered himself onto the chair, sat upright with both feet on the ground and glanced at the clock on the wall. *Wasn't this supposed to start at five o'clock?*

Almost on cue, the facilitator arrived, and the members began introducing themselves, each sharing a grief issue they faced that week. Before long, it became clear to Joe he was not alone in his grief or his pain, and the words poured out of him when his turn arrived to speak.

"Recently, I met a woman who has given me a reason to live. When my wife Kitty died a year ago, I just wanted to die too. But I've been getting better." Joe stood, rocking on his heels, studying the floor.

"Well, um, I thought I was until Saturday night," he said, and shook his head. "We were having so much fun dancing outside under the stars. It felt so good to just tune out, to escape, but when the band played my wife's favorite song, grief came crashing down on me like a gigantic wave and wiped me out. I couldn't breathe. Then something happened. I wrapped my arms around my date like she was a life preserver and hung on to her, and then I could breathe." Joe sniffled. The woman next to him handed him a tissue, and his face turned as pink as his polo shirt. "Thank you," he mumbled.

After everyone had a chance to speak, the presenter introduced herself and spoke about the upcoming weekend grief retreat. She played a video about four people who lost their spouses and how the retreat had helped them to accept their loss and move forward with their lives. Joe felt she was talking directly to him. After the meeting ended, he approached the presenter who was busy organizing her papers.

"That was a great presentation. I was wondering if it's too late to register for the retreat?"

"Not at all. In fact, we just had a cancellation, and there's a private room available," she said, handing him a glossy brochure.

Joe took a deep breath and clenched his fist. "Can I put that on my credit card?"

"Of course. I can do that for you. I'm so glad you can attend. Many attendees have felt this retreat was a life-changing event for them."

"I'm sorry, I've forgotten your name."

"Marjorie McCall."

Joe shook her hand. "Thanks for everything, Marjorie."

As Joe walked out the door, he could feel the stress leaving his body. He knew he made a good decision.

REFLECTION

How many times did Joe show courage?

Brené Brown says, "Courage starts with showing up and letting ourselves be seen." Do you agree? How courageous are you?

ACTION TIP

Become aware of your own courage. At the end of the day, journal about how you demonstrated courage and recognize how brave you were. Ask yourself, "Did I have the courage to make good decisions today?"

PETITION

Dear God,

Please give me the courage to do Your will. In Jesus's name, I pray.

CHAPTER 12

Resilience

On the way home, Joe stopped at the market to grab a few groceries. At the meat counter, he stood in line behind a couple who hemmed and hawed about what to buy. When the husband slid his hand around his wife's waist, a trickle of jealousy moved through Joe, but he dismissed it and wished Joanne were with him. It surprised him that he wasn't wishing for Kitty. He closed his eyes and sighed. Just at that moment his phone beeped with a text message from Joanne: "xxoo." He pressed his lips tight together to keep from smiling as he tapped her a happy face reply.

By the time he arrived home, his stomach was growling with hunger. He started the grill, tossed a few asparagus spears lightly in oil, and seasoned them with sea salt and cracked pepper. When the grill was good and hot, he threw a steak on and set the timer for five minutes. It didn't take long before he caught a whiff of the sizzling steak. He placed his hand on his chest. "Smells great," he said.

Joe glanced around his yard and was shocked to find two shiny eyes peering at him from the woods. His body stiffened.

He wasn't the only one mesmerized by the grilling steak. When Joe stood up for a better view of his uninvited guest, the coyote howled.

"Oh, brother," Joe grumbled. *It's supposed to be a bad omen if a coyote crosses your path.*

Deftly, he flipped the sirloin strip and asparagus spears onto a plate and went into the screened-in porch to have dinner. He was so eager to sink his teeth into the steak, he bit his tongue, and blood oozed out with a metallic taste. "Ow!" he yelled and stomped to the master bathroom to examine the damage.

Approaching the bathroom, a sudden coldness swelled up from his core. Sensing something amiss, he stopped mid stride and heard the sound of footsteps in the hall. From the corner of his eye, he caught a glimpse of someone dressed in black scurrying out the front door. Keeping his wits about him, he slipped his phone out of his pocket and dialed 911. The operator told him not to move or touch anything until the police arrived.

When he saw the destruction to the serene spa space he had shared with Kitty, he cupped his hand over his mouth, unsure if he was going to throw up or have diarrhea or both. The contents of the cabinets, drawers, and closets were tossed about. Glass perfume bottles were smashed to smithereens, their scents mingling in the air. Makeup and nail polish spattered across the white marble floor. Splinters of wood and bits of cracked plaster were everywhere while towels and sheets were strewn across the floor. To add insult to injury, the culprit defecated in the toilet without flushing, and the bathroom stank to high heaven.

Later, after the local police finished the investigation, Officer Curran walked through the house with Joe. Thankfully, nothing else was taken or damaged. Coming back downstairs to the scene of the crime Officer Curran pointed to the toilet and wrinkled his nose. "That's his calling card, and his DNA," he said with compassion in his voice.

Joe rubbed his eyes. "I gotta get out of here."

"Okay, Joe. Let's go out on the porch. I have just a few more questions." His chiseled jaw lifted, and he smiled. With a grimace, Joe dragged himself out and collapsed into a cushioned chair.

Officer Curran had a boyish charm, but in the harshness of the porch light, he looked older.

He turned away and, holding his hands behind his back, began pacing up and down the length of the porch with his dark eyebrows sloping down in a serious expression. Abruptly, he paused and quirked an inquisitive brow. "This was an inside job," he said.

Joe stammered, "What?"

"Well, you know, someone was looking for opioids, and they knew exactly where to find them. Joe, why don't you tell me about the drugs."

"Can I ask you a personal question, officer?"

"Sure."

"Do you have psychic abilities?"

A subtle smile replaced his frown and he said, "Let's just say I have good gut instinct."

Running his hand through his hair, Joe took a couple of deep breaths.

"Well, after Kitty died last year … um, I just never did get around to cleaning out all her stuff." There was a long silence between the two men. Finally, Joe blurted, "Hell, there was an arsenal of pain medication in there!"

"Look, Joe, don't beat yourself up over this. Let's keep moving forward, okay?"

Joe winced. "Yeah."

Officer Curran pulled his notebook out of his breast pocket. "Who knew about Kitty's opioids?"

"No one. No one has been in that bathroom since Kitty died. Except me of course. It's the master bath. There's another bathroom down the hall for guests."

"Think, Joe. Someone knew they were there."

Joe frowned as an awful realization crossed his mind. Turning away, he strode to the bathroom off the foyer. Moments later, with water dripping off his walrus mustache, he walked back to the officer.

"Are you alright, Joe?"

"No." He slumped against the wall. Joe stood there, holding his head in his hands and mumbling, "Oh my God!"

Pinching the bridge of his nose and closing his eyes, Office Curran said, "Talk to me, Joe."

"Alright," Joe sighed. "I hired two cleaning gals. They were here yesterday. Damn—I gave them a key."

"Well, we'll want to talk to them. Got a number?"

Joe reached in his wallet, pulling out the card for D & D House Cleaning.

"Is there someone you can call to be with tonight?"

"Yeah."

"Good." Officer Curran handed him a card for another cleaning service. "Give these folks a call. They are a reputable company and specialize in cleaning up this kind of mess."

As the police drove away, Joe called Joanne.

"Burglarized?" She was shocked. "Open the gate, Joe, I'm on my way."

When Joanne approached Joe's driveway, she pulled off on to the side of the road and grabbed a bottle of mouthwash from her console. After she gargled, she opened the door to spit it out and was astounded to find herself staring into two glowing eyes in the darkness. Catching her breath, she watched as the coyote stepped from behind a tree with a low growl. Joanne screamed, slammed the door, and threw the car into drive, spewing gravel. She made the sign of the cross. *Well, at least I have kissable breath!*

Joe's heart leaped with joy when he heard Joanne at the door. He wrapped his arms around her as he said a little prayer, "Dear God, thank You." He walked her through, showing her the chaotic crime scene, and they ended up in the kitchen where he made her a cup of tea.

She inhaled deeply. "This tea smells so good. Is it spearmint?"

"Yup. So, Jo, how was the drive over?"

"Fine, until I arrived and was nearly devoured by a coyote!"

"A coyote? That could be the same one I saw this evening. Was it scrawny looking?"

"Very," Joanne said. "He had hungry eyes."

"You know, if I hadn't seen that coyote while I was grilling, I might not have come into the house and interrupted the burglar. He might have had time to do more damage." Joe put his hand on his heart. "In a way, I'm grateful for that coyote."

A shadow of concern fell over Joanne's face. "Joe, why don't you start at the beginning and tell me the whole story?"

He took a sip of tea and set his cup down. "I just feel so guilty for keeping those opioids where someone could get at them. What was I thinking?"

"Hey, let go of the guilt. Just tell me the story."

Joe recounted the events up to the departure of the police, then put his feet up on the ottoman. "And there you have it."

Pursing her lips Joanne asked, "Do you know what the D & D stand for in the name of that cleaning company?"

"Well, I assumed it was their names. De—"

"Wait!" Joanne threw her hands up to stop him and said, "Delilah and Dahlia?"

"Yes! That's them!"

Joanne leaped to her feet and began to pace in frustration. "Why would you ever let those two enter your home?"

Joe looked bewildered. "To clean—"

"You are so naive. After an AA meeting, I was in the ladies' room and overheard those two talking about you and how they'd love to help you with your grief."

Joe said, "What the—"

"No! Seriously! One of them said, ' … grief is a great aphrodisiac,' and the other said, 'Joe needs a roll in the hay.'"

His smirk became a huge grin, and then a loud bellowing resounded in the room.

"Joe, it's not funny." She stifled a giggle. "Really, those two are devious divas."

Joe shook his head. "I don't believe it was them, but I bet one of their friends overheard them talking about the drugs they saw in my house. The police will find out when they talk with them."

Joanne fiddled with her pendant, giving Joe a playful grin. "I have an idea."

Joe cocked an eyebrow.

"I think we should go to the AA meeting tomorrow night and have little chat with D & D ourselves."

"You know what I think, Jo? It's time for bed." He picked up her overnight bag, reaching to help her up with his free hand.

Walking down the hall with their fingers intertwined, Joanne shivered as she felt his life energy flow between them. She squeezed tighter to somehow strengthen the connection.

"How's this room?"

Smiling, Joanne assured him it was perfect. He gently leaned in and kissed her. It was a single kiss that said, "I love you in a way that words cannot convey." Then he whispered, "Sweet dreams."

As he turned to leave, Joanne reached for him. "Joe, I want you to know I am so proud of you and how you are dealing with these difficult circumstances."

"Thanks, Jo. That means a lot. You know, sometimes you just have to roll with the punches. Speaking of rolling with the punches, do you mind if I play the piano for a few minutes before I go to bed?" Joe rubbed his neck.

"I'd love it. And it would be a great way to create an oasis of calm after all you've been through. You play all you want."

REFLECTION

Did you notice Joe's resilience? He was able to face and overcome so many problems in his life. Resilience didn't make his problems go away, but it helped him to cope and grow stronger.

How about you? Have you become strengthened by the problems in your life?

ACTION TIP

Accept the things you can't change.

Make a list of things you can't change.

Then make a list of things you *can* change.

Put your effort into one thing you can change.

Everyday choose to believe that things happen for a reason, and it will all turn out for the good. Remember, "This, too, shall pass."

PETITION

Dear God,

Please give me the strength to be resilient and put my trust in You.

CHAPTER 13

Service

oanne toppled into bed. Fumbling around in the dark, she groped for the extra pillow and placed it along side of her body. Pretending it was Joe, she put her arm around it and drifted off to sleep to the sound of the piano's sweet lullaby.

At three in the morning, something woke her from a sound slumber. For half a second, she didn't know where she was. Her eyes flew open wide, and she stared into the darkness, but giddiness overcame her when she remembered she was in Joe's house. Pulling the crisp percale sheets up to her chin, her body squirmed as she suppressed a squeal of joy. Then she jumped out of the bed. On the way back from the bathroom she grabbed her rosary beads from her purse. She crawled back into bed and contemplated all the events that had brought her to this moment. *Imagine, if my heel hadn't gotten stuck in the crack in the sidewalk, I never would have met Joe.* Clasping her hands in prayer, she closed her eyes and thanked God for His orchestrated accident. Before she finished reciting the rosary, a sense of calm engulfed her, and Joanne fell into a deep, peaceful sleep.

When she woke up, the clock read eight thirty. *But how can that be? It's pitch-dark in here.* She pulled the heavy, room-darkening drapes open, and sun flooded the room with a brightness that blinded her for a moment. She blinked but she couldn't believe her eyes. Outside the room was a beautiful terrace overlooking a swimming pool. She opened the sliding glass door and moseyed on out. *This is like a resort.*

After her meditation, she went out to the kitchen. To her relief, the Keurig was sitting on the coffee bar ready to go. In half a jiffy she was sipping a robust cup of coffee out on the front porch. A warmth radiated through her body when she heard the sound of Joe's truck coming up the driveway. She leaned over, rested her elbows on the railing and beamed.

"Hi, Joanne," his deep baritone voice called to her as he hopped down from his truck. Joanne tilted her head back, and her tousled curls bounced. "Morning, Joe," she shouted.

Just as he opened his mouth to speak, his cell phone rang, and they both jumped. He snatched it out of his pocket and stepped onto the porch with his phone to his ear, gesturing to Joanne he'd be right off. When he hung up, he tucked the phone away and sat on the edge of the railing. "Sorry about that. I had to take it," he said. Then he held a white paper bag up in the air and smiled. "Hungry?"

"Mmm, something smells good."

"Fresh out of the oven, whole grain bread."

Joanne rose to her tiptoes and kissed him on his cheek. "Thanks, Joe."

"How 'bout avocado toast?"

"My favorite."

After Joe whipped up breakfast, he motioned Joanne to sit on a stool at the island, and he passed her a plate. She tasted the toast and said, "Delish."

"Hey, Jo. Did you happen to see the note I left for you this morning?"

"Note?" Joanne swallowed. "No, I didn't."

"No big deal. I just wanted you to know where I was when you woke up. Last night, I forgot to mention I usually leave early in the morning to meet my lawn crew at the shop. I like to give them a pep talk before they hit the road." When Joe finished his last bit of toast, he licked his fingers and swiveled his stool to face Joanne. "Let's go out on the front porch."

"Okey dokey." Joanne picked up the plates. "I'm going to throw a few things in the dishwasher, and then I'll join you."

When Joanne went out onto the porch, Joe was rocking in his chair and talking on his cell phone. She curled up in the chair next to him and pulled out her phone to check the new messages.

"Sorry," he said as he hung up. He leaned forward with one hand on his knee. "Do I have a story for you."

Joanne raised her eyebrows. "I'm all ears."

Joe tapped his fingertips together, and he leaned back in the chair. After he cleared his throat, he began to recount the events of the morning.

The day started out like any other day. After he finished his oatmeal and filled a mug with coffee, he settled into his leather desk-chair and began reading his daily devotional. But today something was different. Today the Bible passage jumped off the page. It seemed as if God had a personal message for him. He grinned when he read St. Paul's letter to the Ephesians regarding the thief that no longer steals, but instead labors, doing honest work with his hands, so that he may be able to give to those in need.

As Joe sipped his coffee and pondered the meaning of the reading, he understood what he must do. He always knew that all the money Kitty left to him was never really his. It was God's money. Now, he must find a way to use God's money to help others so they can help themselves. In that moment, his soul woke up, and he felt rejuvenated as his adrenaline rushed through his veins. Joe went off to work with a renewed sense of purpose.

Driving up to the shop, he found a few guys standing outside. They appeared to be having a serious discussion, but when they saw Joe approach, their voices grew hushed. Joe unlocked the door and overheard someone say, "Will he be okay?" At the same moment, Zack swaggered in with a smug look on his face. Taking Joe by the elbow, he led him into the private office and closed the door, flipping his blond hair out of his eyes.

"You gotta get that hair cut," Joe said.

"Yeah, yeah, I know. Listen to this, Joe." He rattled on, repeating the gossip he'd heard at the local coffee house this morning about some guy who had OD'd last night named Kyle Delynks. Zack leaned against the desk with his arms folded and asked, "Does that name ring a bell?"

Joe scratched his head. "Should it?"

"Yeah, that dingbat cleaning lady you hired … Delilah Delynks is his cousin."

"What the hell?"

Zack shrugged. "Ya know what this means?"

"He's the thief!"

"Good guess, Sherlock," Zack said, giving Joe a pat on the back. "Everybody's saying this guy is one lucky bastard."

"How's that?"

"Well, the guy's poor mother found him on the floor and called 911."

"Really?"

"Yeah, he's still in the hospital."

"Thank God," Joe said as he paced the floor.

Kyle was supposed to be discharged from the hospital early in the morning but because of a complication, the doctor decided to keep him a little longer for observation. When Zack finished sharing his news, he headed for the door, but then he stopped and turned. "I can get the guys off to work today. Why don't you go to the hospital?"

Clasping Zack's forearm Joe said, "Thanks, I appreciate your help."

At the hospital, Joe found Kyle laying in a cubical staring at the stained ceiling. There was no TV, not even a chair, in the room. Although Kyle was thirty, he looked thirteen, with his freckled baby face and curly red hair and his worn-out hospital johnny.

Joe attempted to introduce himself, but Kyle crossed his arms over his chest and turned away. "I-I d-don't k-know you," he stammered.

"Ah, but you do," Joe said and looked Kyle directly in the eye. "We met briefly last night ... when you burglarized my home."

Kyle gave Joe an incredulous stare.

"How long do you think it's going to take the police to put two and two together? I'm surprised they're not walking in here right now."

With a clenched jaw, Kyle slouched down in the bed, pulled the threadbare covers up, and shivered. "It's friggin' freezin' in here."

"Yeah, it's as cold as a meat locker. So, how did you get to the end of your rope?"

"You want to know how, huh?"

"Yeah, I do."

For a brief moment, it was so quiet you could hear a pin drop. Then Kyle rubbed his hands together, cracked his knuckles, and began to explain how he became addicted to drugs.

"Five years ago, I had a great wife and a great job. Heck, five years ago I had a great life." Kyle's voice started to crack. "There was an accident."

"Hmm." Joe handed him a tissue.

Kyle had fallen off a scaffold at a construction site and suffered a fractured leg and a broken arm. He was confined to his home for ten weeks. Before long, he was hooked on pain killers, and eventually the drugs took over his mind. He lost everything.

By the time he finished his story, the tissue was shredded.

As Joe dug around in the box on the table for more tissues, he said, "You know, Kyle, sometimes we have to lose everything to find Christ."

In a brittle voice, Kyle said, "Don't give me that crap. I've had it! I ain't going on livin' like a rat. I ain't afraid to die."

"Kyle, I can help you."

"Don't you get it, mister?" he yelled, "I don't want your friggin' help."

"Okay, relax. I'm just saying, you deserve a second chance."

"Well, sometimes goodbye is a second chance.'"

Joe clasped his hands together. "Please, don't give up, Kyle." No one said a word for several seconds. The silence was broken by the sound of someone snoring on the other side of the curtain.

Kyle threw Joe an exasperated look.

"It sounds like a rusty chainsaw cutting through Styrofoam over there."

Kyle's burst of laughter cleared the tension in the air.

"I wish I could make this mess disappear, but it's out of my hands," Joe said. "You see, Kyle, the police are involved." Joe blew out his cheeks. "But don't worry, now the court system has a new method of dealing with drug-related offenses. It's called the drug court. Since you don't have a record, I believe you qualify. I'm praying you do." Joe's eyes darted to the shadow of a cross on the wall behind Kyle's bed. He stiffened a moment. "In order for you to get started, you need a lawyer. I called a friend, and she has agreed to represent you with the police and the district attorney. She'll do what she can to get you qualified for the drug court." Joe glanced at the time. "Her name is Michaela, and she should be here any minute."

Kyle's red eyebrows squished together. "I don't have money for a lawyer."

"I'm paying her to represent you." Joe smiled.

"Are … are you sure?" Kyle asked.

"Yup."

"Why would you do this for me?"

"Kyle, forty-five years ago, I was just like you. I, uh, was a thief and an addict."

Kyle looked at Joe and corked his head. "Are you kidding?"

"No. When I got caught, someone gave me a second chance. Now it's my turn to help someone help themselves. I believe God put you on my path for a reason."

Kyle gave Joe a questioning look.

"If the court agrees to rehab for you, and if you follow all the procedures and regulations of the treatment facility, they'll inform the court and all criminal charges against you will be dropped. What do you say to a second chance?"

Picking lint from his hospital blanket, Kyle was silent. Joe leaned against the wall with his thumbs in the front pockets of his jeans and waited. Finally, Kyle tilted his head toward Joe. For the first time, Joe noticed something in Kyle's pale blue eyes. It was a childlike innocence.

"Okay," he said.

Joe reached across the bed and shook Kyle's hand. "I'm here for you." As he walked away, he stopped and turned around. "Hey, Kyle, when you get out, I've got a job waiting for you."

REFLECTION

Did you notice how energized Joe became when he felt he had a sense of purpose? Whenever you can serve someone, do it. Don't pass up the opportunity. God gave you gifts, talents, and resources, so use them with passion to serve someone.

ACTION TIP

Think of ways you can serve someone this week. Make a list of people you can serve. If you can't think of ways to serve, go online. There are hundreds of things you can do. Choose one today. The best way to serve is to do so humbly, expecting nothing in return.

Imagine, Jesus was the son of God, and yet He wasn't too proud to wash the feet of His disciples. He did it as an example for us. What is something you are too proud to do? What activity do you consider to be beneath you? You could start by giving someone a second chance.

PETITION

Dear God,

How can I serve You today? Who do You want me to serve? Please help me to use all the gifts You have blessed me with to serve others and You.

CHAPTER 14

Forgiveness

After Joe summarized the morning events, Joanne said, "Wow, you amaze me." With her elbow, she gave him a playful nudge. "Hey, how is it possible to forgive someone who demolished your bathroom?"

Joe chuckled. "Jesus challenges us to forgive the unlovable. In the gospel of Matthew, He says if you forgive, God will forgive you, but if you don't forgive, God will not forgive you. Every day I pray for the grace to forgive. Forgiveness is the key to my happiness."

Joe shuffled his feet as he stared at the ground. "I'm no saint. Forgiveness is something I do for myself. It doesn't mean I excuse his actions. When I forgive, I release resentment, blame, and pain. You know why?"

Joanne blinked. "Why?"

"I let it all go to make room in my heart for love."

Joanne crossed her arms. "Well, it's not easy for me to forgive. I torment myself with consuming, crazy notions. The more I ruminate, the more I realize …" *Shut up, Joanne. He's going to think you're whacked.*

"Listen, Jo, the power to change is in you. Ask God to help you let go of all the unforgiveness you buried inside. Those suppressed emotions take up way too much space in your heart."

"You're right."

With one finger, Joe caressed her cheek. "You must feel your feelings to heal. Then when you do, turn them over to God … all the shame, blame, pain. Let them all go so there's plenty of room in your beautiful heart for my love."

She smiled. "How can I thank you for your sound advice?"

"Well, funny you ask because I need a favor."

"You do?"

Joe stepped back and placed a hand on his hip.

"Yup," he said. "With all the commotion last night, I forgot to mention I signed up to go on a grief support retreat this week."

"That's wonderful."

"Would you be able to stay here for a couple of days? The cleaning company is scheduled to start the restoration of my master bathroom on Friday. I think the job needs to be supervised." He shook his head. "Don't you agree?"

"Definitely! How long will you be gone?"

"Thursday till Sunday. How would you like to be my project manager?"

"Sure."

"Thanks, Jo." He wrapped his arms around her in a body-crushing hug. She rubbed his back and stepped back.

"Gosh," she said as she glanced at the time. "Gotta dash."

"Hey, what's your hurry?" Joe asked.

"Oh, there's so much to do. I need to prepare for my new client, pack some clothes, pick up my pills …"

Joe raised his bushy eyebrows. "Whoa, pills?"

"Yes, I take heart medication."

"What's wrong with your heart?"

"Well, back in the day, when I was getting off the booze, I, um … well, during the withdrawal from the alcohol, I experienced violent d.t.'s and suffered a massive heart attack."

"What?" he gasped.

Joanne glanced at Joe with a mischievous gleam in her eye as she twirled a curl around her finger.

"I'm fine now."

Under her bravado, Joe sensed a fragility about Joanne.

"Thank God you're all right," he said.

"Uh-huh, I'm grateful to be alive."

He placed a hand on his chest. "I'm grateful too."

"The heart attack was a gift from God."

"Are you kidding?" Joe asked.

"No. After I left the hospital, I experienced a shift in my perception and became aware of a new purpose for living. God used the heart attack to get my attention—to bring me back to Him—and He placed an ache in my heart to lead others to Him."

"I envy you, Joanne. What's more fulfilling than helping people heal their pain and develop a personal relationship with God?"

"Joe, it's never too late to start over again. You inspire people. Have you ever considered being a coach?"

"Me? A coach?"

"Yes, why not?"

Joe glanced around as if looking for an answer. Instead he said, "Well, not to change the subject, but what's up with your client tonight?"

"Oddly enough, she's dealing with my biggest stumbling block. Forgiveness," she said.

"Oh," Joe said. "Did you ever hear the quote by Richard Bach?"

"Never heard of him."

"'We teach best what we most need to learn.'"

"Wow. How do you know that?"

"He is one of my favorite authors. His stories are filled with inspiration." Joe took Joanne's hands and teased, "Pleeease, stay for quick lunch and dip in the pool before you leave?"

As she shifted from foot to foot, she jiggled her keys. "Not today, I'm late." *Not today or any day is he going to see me in my skimpy tankini with all my fat bulging out.*

She rushed out of Joe's house, half-walking, half-running, and jumped in her car. "Bye-bye!" she yelled as she drove off.

With the top down and her sunglasses on she started her long ride home. As she drove along, she hit the select button and found a contemporary Christian radio station. She turned up the volume and sang along, but it was as if her heart and soul sang the words. Then she recalled how the words of scripture she had read that morning had touched her: I pray that the eyes of your heart would be enlightened. She cried out, "Lord, please open the eyes of my heart. I want to be aware of Your presence every day."

While she was cruising down the highway, her conscious mind wandered off, thinking about bathing suits, and her subconscious mind drove her to the mall.

She spotted it as soon as she walked in the store. It was like love at first sight. When she ripped the bathing suit off the rack, she was shocked at the price. *Oh well, if it fits, I am getting it.*

She hurried into the dressing room to try it on. At first, she struggled and wiggled and jiggled, but finally she pulled the swimsuit on without snagging a nail. *Wow.* A smile crept across her face. With her hands on her hips and her chin held high, she looked in the three-way mirror. Somehow, she appeared ten pounds lighter.

Joanne jumped when she heard a loud knock on the dressing room door.

"It's just me," said the saleslady. "Do you need any help?"

Joanne opened the door. "Thanks, I'm all set."

"Honey, you just discovered the perfect style suit for your body, and the turquoise hue is stunning on you."

"Thank you," said Joanne, "but are these trick mirrors?"

"No, absolutely not! You look marvelous. Wait here, I'll be right back." She disappeared but was back in a flash with a coordinating, sexy sarong. "Try this on," she suggested.

Joanne wrapped it around her waist and spun around with her arms in the air. In a soft voice she whispered, "Thank You, God." While looking in the mirror she said, "I behold you, my beautiful body. I'm sorry for criticizing you. Please forgive me. I love you. I thank you and I am grateful for all you do for me." Joanne stepped a bit closer to the mirror. She gazed deep into her eyes. "I see you in there my beautiful soul. I am sorry for abusing you and for all the times I hurt you. Please forgive me. I love you. I thank you, and I am grateful for your love."

When Joanne came out of the dressing room, the saleslady said, "Today's your special day, sweetie. All the suits are half price."

Joanne peered into the woman's eyes. "Yes, today is my special day, and you are special too. Thank you."

Arriving at home, Joanne discovered a white paper stuffed in her door. To her dismay, it was her rental renewal and a notice of a rent increase. *No way can I pay that.* She flopped down at her desk and held her head in her hands.

To relieve her stress, she decided to treat her body and soul to a luxurious bath in her soaker tub. By adding bath salts to the water, she enhanced the relaxing experience and soothed her senses with the scent of lavender. With her exfoliating glove, she scrubbed away the dead skin cells along with her anxiety over her rent.

Stepping out of the tub, Joanne noticed her skin was now radiant and smooth. As fast as she slathered on a super-hydrating body moisturizer, it was absorbed. After she slipped into her pink robe and platform flip-flop sandals, she grabbed her phone and strutted out to the porch. Just as she was about to sit, her phone rang, and she saw on the screen it was Greg from the real estate office. "Hi, Greg," she said. "I was just going to call you."

"Oh?"

"The thing is," said Joanne. "I won't be available for the rest of the week."

"I was just doing our schedule, so I'll work that in. Take care."

REFLECTION

The meaning of the word forgive is to stop feeling angry or resentful toward someone.

How often have you said, "I forgive you" but hold on to resentment in your heart? Do you see how you are hurting yourself?

ACTION TIP

To truly forgive someone takes prayer and continual surrender to God. Set yourself free by asking for God's help. Write a letter to someone who has hurt you. Tell them how they hurt you and how you feel. Get it all off your chest. Let it rip! Even if the person is dead, release all your pain on paper. After you let it all out, burn the letter or shred it.

Remember, hurt people hurt people. When someone causes you pain, it is not about you, but it is about their own pain. Try to understand where they are coming from.

PETITION

Dear God,

Will You please help me to forgive as You do? Please open the eyes of my heart. Let me see You in everyone I meet. Help me to let go of all the pain and resentment. Please set me free!

CHAPTER 15

Self-forgiveness

t five o'clock the doorbell chimed. Standing there hugging herself, Bambi was dressed in a slim, black pencil skirt and a crisp, white sleeveless blouse with a wide, red patent-leather belt wrapped around her tiny waist. Wearing high-waisted jeans, a floral shirt, and a big smile, Joanne greeted Bambi.

"This is lovely," Bambi said as she stepped through the door. "I like your style."

"Oh, thank you." At first glance, Joanne almost laughed. Bambi resembled Walt Disney's Bambi, with her big doe eyes and long, spindly legs. "Please, sit down and make yourself comfortable. Can I get you a water?"

"Sure, but may I have it in a glass, please?"

"Of course. I'll be right back."

Bambi crumpled into the comfy chair and fidgeted with a white lace hanky. She hadn't had a drink all week. *I would give anything for a beer right now.*

Joanne grabbed a bottle of water from the fridge and poured some into a crystal wine glass. "Here you go," she said.

Bambi gripped the glass and took a sip. "Oh, how nice." She leaned her head back and squeezed her eyes shut. "Thanks," she murmured.

Joanne peered over the rim of her reading glasses to get a better look at Bambi's long, thick eyelashes. *I wonder if they're real.*

"Bambi, I love your stylized pixie hairdo."

"Thank you," she said with a knowing look. "I cut and color it myself."

"Well, it suits you."

She gave Joanne a tight-lipped smile to conceal the gap between her front teeth. "You know, when my mother became ill, I let myself go," she said with a big sigh. "I let go of my job, my boyfriend, my whole life to become her caretaker." One lone tear rolled down her cheek as she recalled the night her mother died. The doctor informed her the end was near, but it didn't come right away. Day after day, night after night, Bambi stayed by her mother's side. One night, exhausted from sitting vigil in the hospital, Bambi snuck home to catch a few hours of sleep, and while she slept, her mother slipped away. Tears welled in her eyes as she shared her story. "She died alone!" Bambi swiped at her nose with her scrunched-up hanky and sobbed, "If only I didn't leave."

Joanne passed a box of tissues to Bambi, but she knocked it out of her hands as she grasped her forearm and pleaded, "Please, help me."

Joanne squeezed her hand. In a gentle tone she said, "I am so sorry for your pain."

Bambi covered her face with her hands and, with a cracking voice, said, "I can't forgive myself for leaving her alone." Her chin quivered and her eyes glistened as she continued to talk about her mother. "You see, Joanne, my mother was right. She always said I was selfish. Even when I was just a little girl, she called me selfish. My whole life I heard her say, 'You are so self-centered.'" Bambi pulled some tissue out of the box and blew her nose. "I tried so hard to prove her wrong, but she was right. She was always right." She sniffled and began to cry.

Joanne's leather chair squeaked when she leaned forward to rub Bambi's back. "Just breathe," she whispered. Then Joanne cleared her throat. "From my life experience, I've noticed parents with good intentions call their children selfish in an attempt to control their behavior. Making a child feel guilty is one way a parent can insure the child will obey them."

Bambi said, "That old guilt trip." She stood and shuddered. "May I use your bathroom?"

"Of course!" Joanne pointed the way.

While Bambi was in the bathroom, Joanne closed her eyes and prayed for the words to say. She knew how Bambi suffered. Her own mother told her she was selfish too. Those guilt trips paved the way to her self-destructive path. Being told she was selfish made her feel undeserving of forgiveness until she felt God's unconditional love. Now God was using her to help Bambi.

When Bambi walked back from the bathroom, she perched herself on the edge of the chair and gripped her phone. Tapping her polished red nails against the screen, she checked her messages.

"Bambi, please shut your phone off."

"Sorry, I just needed to check a message."

"Well, that's not possible right now. You need to focus on you." Joanne let out a loud exhale and continued. "Checking your phone is sending me a message that your phone is more important than our meeting. And that is not cool." Joanne folded her arms. "Your mother used the word 'selfish' to control you, and now you're allowing her to continue to control you from the grave. Bambi, you're angry with your mother for dying alone, and you resent her for not waiting for you to be there. But now it's time to let it go. When you forgive your mother, you will set yourself free. If you start today to love yourself a little bit more, it will be easier to forgive yourself."

Bambi rubbed her forehead and asked, "What's wrong with me? Ever since my mother passed, I can't think straight. I feel like I'm lost in space."

Joanne crossed her legs. "That's a good way to describe what you're going through," Joanne said in a soothing tone. "With the loss of your mother you have entered a liminal space. Father Richard Rohr describes it as 'Where we are betwixt and between the familiar and the completely unknown.'"

Bambi slouched in the chair. As she jiggled her leg up and down, her black mule slipped off her foot and flew across the room. She bolted from the chair to retrieve it. "Sorry. See what I mean? I'm up in the air."

Joanne took a breath, counted to five, and gathered her thoughts. "Liminal comes from the Latin root limen meaning threshold. See, Bambi, you are standing at a threshold. This is a good time for you to stop and rest because you are too exhausted to go further."

"That's for sure," said Bambi.

"Once you surrender to this space, you can relax and just be in the moment. Spending time in meditation and silence will help you to get to know your true self and connect with God. Something wonderful is waiting for you. Take time to search your soul and find your true self. This is the time to say goodbye to what was and hello to what will be."

Bambi mumbled, "I don't know how to meditate."

"Don't you worry. I'll teach you. This is your sacred time … time to forgive yourself."

Bambi smiled and didn't attempt to hide her gap.

"For your homework this week, I want you to consider the words inspired by John of the Cross, 'Love what God sees in you.'"

"I'll try."

"Every day, write down three things you love about yourself."

Looking down, Bambi said, "Oh, come on."

"Also, write an essay about all the benefits you receive by forgiving yourself."

Bambi let out an impatient huff. "Look, Joanne, I'm not good at writing," she said with a grimace.

"I'm not going to be examining your handwriting." She glanced at her notes. "Also, I want you to write an essay on all the benefits you receive by not forgiving yourself."

"Oh, God, if only I could write better." Bambi pulled at her short hair and it stuck up in the air.

"Stop with the 'if only' right now. Do you know those two little words can steal your joy?"

"Well, thank you for listening to me. I'm such a blabbermouth. My mother must be rolling over in her grave," she said and threw her bag over her shoulder.

"Hey, no cutting yourself down. You have to start building yourself up."

"I know," she said as she got up to leave.

"So, are you ready to stop saying 'if only' and start saying, 'what's next?'"

Bambi stood silent for a moment, then she said, "Yes, I am ready!"

Joanne turned to her. "Here's my card, please call if you

need me. Let's schedule a session next week. Same day, same time, on time."

Bambi gave her a kiss on the cheek. "Thank you," she said and glanced at her phone.

"You seem to have a compulsion to check your phone. Be careful, it can be addictive."

"Oh no, I don't have a problem."

"Just be careful. Until you learn to forgive yourself, guilt can fester and turn into a bad habit or vice and even poor health. Also, when you're all tied up on the internet, you aren't free to develop your relationship with God."

Bambi shot Joanne a curious look. "I get the impression you've had your share of addiction. Is that true?"

"Okay, that's true … booze, drugs, sex, food, shopping, self-improvement courses, you name it. I was always trying to stay numb so I couldn't feel the pain of not forgiving myself."

"Oh gosh, I'm sorry," said Bambi. "I don't have a filter."

"Don't worry. No need to apologize," Joanne said as she opened the door. "Don't apologize for being yourself."

REFLECTION

Self-forgiveness is not easy or comfortable. In fact, it may be the hardest thing you ever do, but you can do it. It takes time. When you learn to forgive yourself, your whole world gets better. You are worth the effort.

ACTION TIP

Your mistakes are your best teachers. Learn from them. This week, set aside some time to pray, to spend time in silence, and meditate. Make a vow not to repeat your mistakes.

It takes courage to admit your flaws; sometimes talking with someone helps. Confession is good for the soul.

Write a letter to yourself and unburden your heart. List all the reasons you struggle to forgive yourself. No one needs to read your letter. You can burn it.

PETITION

Dear God,

I am truly sorry for not forgiving myself. Please, will You give me the grace to be able to forgive myself as You forgive me. Thank You for loving me.

CHAPTER 16

Acceptance

On Saturday, the restoration company finished the job and restored Joe's master bathroom to its original beauty. But on Sunday morning, the lingering smell of the fresh paint woke Joanne up from a fitful sleep. When she sniffed it, her stomach lurched, and she decided it was best if she returned to her own apartment to get ready for Joe.

She dawdled the day away, counting the minutes until Joe returned. To ensure she didn't smudge her perfectly applied hot-pink lipstick, she slurped a berrylicious smoothie down to the last drop through a straw. When she rechecked her makeup and hair in the mirror, she discovered a dribble of the delicious drink dripped down her chin and stained her new, white, eyelet dress. She screamed, "Oh no!" Panic seized her. She dashed to her bedroom and frantically rummaged through the closet, hoping to find a fun sundress to wear on this hot August afternoon.

In desperation, she groped in the back of the closet and plucked a funky dress off the "just-in-case" rack. She never dreamed she'd squeeze into it again, but when she stepped into the yellow and white polka-dot, peplum dress, it fit like a glove. She slipped on her white sling-back heels and strutted around the room, thrusting her fist in the air. Then she knelt and raised her arms. "Thank You, Lord!"

Her phone rang and she snatched it, but when she glanced at the time, she declined the call and threw the phone in her purse. *Oh my gosh, it's late.* She dashed out of her apartment, pounded down the hall, and sprinted to her car in the parking lot. When she hopped into her red convertible, she slipped on her white sunglasses and popped a white straw hat on her head to keep the relentless sun off her face. Then she dropped the top, revved the engine, and sped away.

Cruising down the highway, she cranked up the radio, and as she bopped to the music, she belted out the lyrics to the songs. The faint flutters in her tummy expanded, and as a wave of euphoria flooded her, she clutched her heart. After the sensation intensified, Joanne couldn't contain the joy another moment, and a loud shout burst out of her at the top of her lungs, "Woo-hoo!"

Somehow, in all the excitement, Joanne's foot slid out of her sling-back heel and off the gas pedal. Her convertible veered to the other lane and almost collided with an oncoming pickup. When the truck driver laid on his horn, Joanne's face turned death white, and her heart raced. She attempted to turn out of the way, but when she gripped the steering wheel, it slipped out of her wet hands. She wiped her sweaty palms on her pretty dress. *Phew! That was a close call. Thank You, dear God.*

By the time she pulled into the church parking lot, her heart hammered louder than the idling Mercedes engine. She shut the car off and surveyed the parking options. A few cars scattered the lot, but no minivan in sight. She let out a huge exhale and titled her head back to look at the sky. Trying to calm herself, she watched the puffy white clouds roll by and breathed in and out through her nose, but when an eagle soared across the blue sky, she held her breath. A balmy breeze brushed her face, and the words to the hymn "On Eagles Wings" unexpectedly dropped into her consciousness. Memories flooded back to the day of her mother's funeral, and the words to the song touched her.

Just then, a yellow minibus bounced onto the gravel driveway next to the church hall, trailing a cloud of dust. The bus screeched to a stop, and Joanne saw the passengers stand up and squeeze down the aisle, but she didn't see Joe.

After everyone stepped out and rolled their luggage away, one couple stood chatting, but no Joe. Joanne perceived an emptiness in the pit of her stomach. *Where the heck is he?* She rubbed her arms and hugged herself. The stunning woman dressed in a structured black-and-white sheath dress waved to her and strutted into the hall. Joanne watched the well-dressed gentleman pass a card to the minibus driver. He wore a handsome straw fedora, khaki slacks, and a classic, blue button-down shirt. Something about him was familiar. She picked up her phone and called Joe.

"Where are you?"

"Right here."

"Where?"

"One of the wheels on my rolling luggage broke off. I'm dragging it behind me across the parking lot."

Joanne threw the phone down, swung her feet out of the car, and leaped into Joe's arms. "Where's your mustache?"

"I left it at the retreat center, along with a lot of stuff. I'll tell you all about it when we get home," he said as he tossed his suitcase in the back seat. Joanne pulled her sunglasses off and glared at Joe.

"Why are you staring at me?" he asked.

"You look so different. I really didn't recognize you."

Joe grinned. "Is that a good thing or a bad thing?"

"It's all good. You look ten years younger."

"I feel ten years younger too."

Joanne reached up and placed her arms around his neck. She leaned back and gave him a come-hither look. "Can I kiss your mustache-less lips?"

Joe roared with laughter.

She grabbed his hat off his head and flung it in the backseat. Then she ran her fingers softly through his hat hair and kissed him on his warm lips. "Mmm, nice."

When Joe put his arms around her, she backed up. "Hey, let's not get carried away in the church parking lot."

Joe chuckled. "Right. Let's get out of here."

Joanne fished Joe's hat out of the back seat and plonked it on his head as they drove away.

Parking her car in front of Joe's bungalow, a warmth radiated through her body. She hugged herself to hold it in and smiled at Joe. "Ah," she said. "Home."

Joe's eyes crinkled at the corners. "I like the way you say 'home.'" He unbuckled the seatbelt and squirmed in his seat to face her. When he took her hand, he intertwined his fingers with hers. For a moment, Joe's eyes dug into Joanne then he drew in a deep breath. "Would you consider moving in with me?" he blurted out. "You don't have to answer me right now, I know it's a lot to absorb." He paused and smiled. "Of course, you'll have your own suite."

Joanne's pulse quickened.

"While I was away, did you walk around the grounds or go down by the pond?" Joe asked.

"No, why?"

"Let's go for a stroll," he said. "You'll see why."

"Okay, but I need to change into my flip-flops to walk around."

As they approached Kitty's derelict backyard garden, Joanne gripped Joe's arm. "Oh my gosh! It's been restored to its former glory."

Window boxes filled with lavender hung from the freshly painted potting shed, and when Joanne brushed by them, they released their fragrance. As she surveyed the revitalized enchanted garden, she stretched her arms and twirled around. With a baffled expression on her face, she looked at Joe. "How is this possible?"

Joe shrugged and gave her a playful grin. "Just like any transformation, by taking baby steps every day, one day at a time."

"I am mystified," she said. "Last time I saw this place, it was a disgrace. I almost cried, it was a neglected mess … weeds, dead plants, debris everywhere."

"Before Kitty became ill, she didn't allow my landscape crew in her garden. She loved caring for it herself."

"Really?"

"Kitty always said, 'Working in my garden makes my soul shine.' After she died, I couldn't come near here," he mumbled. "I'm grateful for the way Zack and his crew tackled the task."

"Did you notice the shine on the granite bench?" Joanne asked.

"Yup. It was restored professionally."

As she stepped closer, she clasped her hands behind her back and glanced down to see "Kitty's Place" etched in the stone. She caught her breath in a startled gasp and clasped Joe's hand.

"Let's take a seat." Looking down with an unfocused stare, Joe sat quietly.

Joanne rested her hand on his knee and took a deep breath. *What a great place to meditate.*

"You know what I learned at the retreat?"

"What?"

"The cure for grief is to keep the memory of the loved one alive."

She listened to the rustling of the trees and wondered what he meant by those words.

Joe stood and shuffled his feet on the new brick walkway. "The retreat center was nice, but it couldn't compare to this," he said as he spread his arms.

Joanne closed her eyes. "This is heavenly!"

"Yeah, it is. It's a great spot. At the retreat I experienced an enormous breakthrough, and I received profound insight about this place."

Joanne patted a spot next to her on the granite bench. "Sit here and tell me about it," she said as she scooted over.

Joe pulled a protein bar out of his back pocket. "Want some?"

"No, thanks."

He took a bite. "Ah, dark chocolate." After he gobbled it up, he licked his lips and nestled next to her. Without any warning, he leaned over and kissed her forehead. "I love you," he said. He wrapped his arms around her and kissed her softly on her lips.

"Mmm," she said. "Chocolatey."

When he reached over and brushed a curl out of her eyes, she whispered, "I love your chocolate kisses and I love you too."

"Joanne," he said with a yearning look. "What am I going to do with you?"

"Joe, can you stop right there?" Joanne jumped up. "Sorry

to interrupt but this bench is killing my butt. Let's sit on the veranda?"

"Yeah!" Joe arched his back. "I know what you mean," he said.

They strolled hand in hand along the brick walkway. When they reached the porch, Joanne yelled out, "Here we are!"

She ran to the top step, and as she twirled around, a slight breeze blew up her dress, giving Joe a glimpse of her teeny, yellow, polka-dot bikini undies.

Joe rubbed his index finger across where his mustache used to be. "It's amazing how you look like Marilyn Monroe in that dress today."

She beamed. "Well, thank you, Joe." Joanne winked at him and flopped on the cushioned chaise longue. "Ah," she said. "This is more like it. Now where were you in your story?"

"Sorry, I guess I got a little distracted." He closed his eyes as he recalled the events that happened at the grief retreat.

On the first night after dinner, the guest speaker spoke about managing grief through journaling, leaving the audience speechless. Tears welled in Joe's eyes, but he refused to cry. He listened without judgment. As he headed to his room, his grief counselor stopped him in the hall and placed a notebook and pen in his hands.

"Your assignment tonight," he said, "I want you to write a letter to Kitty."

"We'll see," Joe said and stifled a yawn.

"Believe me, Joe, you'll thank me tomorrow."

He unlocked the door to his room and threw the notebook and pen on the desk. When he crumpled into the chair at the desk, he became aware of a tightening in his chest. *Why the hell did I ever agree to come here?* He leaned back and placed both hands behind his head and massaged his neck. Daunted by the idea of writing to Kitty, he slouched in the chair and stared into space. Finally, he took a deep breath and cried out, "Come, Holy Spirit, please illuminate my mind and instruct me in what to write. Please help me!"

He picked up the pen and put it down again. He closed his eyes and waited for inspiration, but the pain in his neck intensified and took his attention away. After he focused on his breathing, the pain diminished. When he started writing, the words flowed. His jumbled thoughts and feelings tumbled out on paper, expressing the suppressed tension he endured as Kitty's caregiver, his anger with her for leaving him, his deep resentment for his own helplessness, and his buried hate and fear of the disease.

The more he wrote, the better he felt. Journaling, he discovered, was an incredible tool for catharsis. It allowed Joe to release repressed emotions and painful memories, freeing his mind to ponder new possibilities. After writing for about forty-five minutes, Joe detected no pain in his neck. A surge of gratitude overwhelmed him. Although he hadn't prayed on his knees since he was a little boy, he knelt and raised his arms. "Here, Lord, I release all my emotional baggage to You. I let go and I accept Your will. Thy will be done. Thank You!"

He climbed into bed exhausted by his emotional turmoil, but sleep eluded him. Tossing and turning, he contemplated ways to keep Kitty's memory alive.

"As I was tossing and turning, the idea popped into my head."

"What idea?"

"How to keep Kitty's memory alive."

"How?"

Leaning back in the rocking chair, Joe placed his hands

behind his head and said, "I decided to convert Kitty's estate into our retreat center."

"Our … retreat center?" she screeched.

"Yup!"

Joanne hopped up from the chaise longue and held out her arms as if to hug the world. "Omigosh," she screamed. "I can't believe it."

Joe stood and took her hands, pulling her into his arms. She rested her head on his chest and they swayed. Joanne looked up into his eyes. "I have an idea, Joe."

"What's that?"

"How about we call our retreat center, Kitty's Place?"

Joe lifted Joanne up and swung her around as tears rolled down his face.

REFLECTION

Acceptance is what it takes to live life without fighting against it. It stops the constant battle and struggle. Remember what we resist, persists. Once you accept your past, you can change your future.

Did you notice how Joe was able to move forward in life once he accepted Kitty's death? Acceptance transformed his life.

ACTION TIP

Journaling helped Joe, and it can help you too. Take a few moments every day this week and write about acceptance. What does acceptance mean to you? What painful situation do you need to accept right now? What situation have you accepted, and how has acceptance helped you? Notice how you suffer when you refuse to accept a situation.

Spend a few moments in meditation. Just be in the present moment and watch how it allows you to accept what is.

PETITION

Dear God,

Please grant me the serenity to accept the things I cannot change.

CHAPTER 17

Trusting God

n the day Joanne moved in with Joe, he sold his landscape company. Together they began the task of launching the retreat center. By collaborating, they made their dream a reality.

The website designer showcased the beauty of the property and captured the essence of the retreat experience. With an impactful and innovative marketing campaign, the rooms were booked until the end of December. They planned to vacation in Florida for the winter and reopen Kitty's Place in the spring.

To accommodate the staff, the backyard barn was converted into what they called a "barndominium." Zack became the general contractor and immediately acquired the building permits to get the construction underway.

Bambi, as it turned out, had a degree in nutrition. When she applied for the position of head chef, Joanne's gut said yes. She hired her on the spot, and Bambi moved into her room as soon as it was completed.

Joanne and Joe refused to let discouraging remarks about starting a retreat center daunt their dreams. They trusted God to provide the stamina for the work He called them to do. Every morning they prayed together, and soon they stopped asking God for what they wanted and instead started asking Him for what He wanted.

One night after dinner as Joe played the piano, Joanne leaped from her chair.

"Joe! Stop for a minute, I just got an idea." Her eyes sparkled and gleamed when she asked, "What do you think if we incorporate your music into the retreat program?"

"What do you mean?"

"Well, you know how when you play at the end of the day, the music lifts us up?"

"Yeah."

"Wouldn't it be a great way to end a day of retreat? After the evening meal, everyone could gather in the piano room to hear you play. Music is a wonderful way to bring people together, and it would sooth their souls before they go to bed."

Joe gave her a wide grin and said, "Let's do it!"

One sunny afternoon, Joanne took a break from preparing for the grand opening. Outside on the veranda, as she rocked away, the sun warmed her closed eyelids, and she daydreamed about transforming the summer porch into a fall retreat with curb appeal.

Just then, Joe clomped up the front-porch stairs in his chunky work boots and startled Joanne. There he stood with a humongous pumpkin on his shoulder and a huge grin on his face.

"Oh, my goodness! That thing must weigh fifty pounds."

Joe chuckled. "There's more."

Joanne bounced down the stairs squealing, "Let's see!" She stood on her tiptoes and peered into the bed of the truck. Jerking her head back, she glared at Joe with a skeptical expression.

"What?" he asked.

"Why is there a pumpkin patch in the back of your truck?"

Joe squinted and tipped his cowboy hat. "You'll see."

"Need any help unloading?"

"No, thanks," he said as he scooped up a bunch of pumpkins. "No sense you getting dirty." Joe jostled the pumpkins together in his arms and headed up the front walkway. Just as he reached the front stairs, he stumbled, and a big pumpkin dropped and splattered all over the place.

Joanne laughed so hard; tears ran down her face.

Joe bent over and held his sides as though he had a stomachache. He chortled, "What do you call a pumpkin that gets dropped?"

"A mess?"

"Nope … a squash."

"Ha ha ha!" Joanne dissolved into a puddle of giggles. Joe held her shoulders to keep them from shaking. When he kissed her, a smile flashed across her face.

"Sorry, Joe."

"Don't be sorry. The sound of your laughter transports me away." Joe pulled her close, but she leaned back.

Looking in Joe's eyes paralyzed her for a moment. Then she sighed and said, "We better clean up this mess."

After Joe finished decorating the porches and the terrace, he dressed up the front stairs with potted mums. He placed a fall wreath on the front door and Joanne beamed.

"Just the extra oomph it needed."

"Let's take a stroll down to the pond." Joe suggested.

"Are you kidding? We have a ton of work."

"It can wait. Come on, we won't have many more days like this."

"Yeah, you're right. Summer is coming to a screeching halt."

Arriving at the meandering path, they discovered it was covered with leaves. "Take my hand," Joe said. "I'll guide you."

"What's that noise?" she asked.

Joe whipped around looking up into the trees. "It's just Mr. Woodpecker."

"Wow! Look how the leaves whirl and twirl without making a sound. Mr. Woodpecker could learn a lesson from them."

"These trees can teach us all a few lessons on how to let go."

A wave of grief engulfed Joanne as the dry leaves crunched under her feet. The musty, earthy smell of their decay assaulted her nostrils, and a bitter bile burned in her throat, triggering painful autumn memories of long ago.

Joanne skipped ahead and climbed the hill to get a better view of the meadow across the way.

"Hey, Joe." She called over her shoulder. "There's a sea of yellow flowers blowing in the breeze."

Joe caught up with her. "That's goldenrod, a late bloomer."

"Goldenrod? Doesn't that cause hay fever?"

"Nope, it's a non-allergenic plant, but it gets a bum rap because it blooms the same time of year as the real culprit—ragweed."

"Really?"

"Yup, every year I'm plagued by ragweed pollen."

"You are?"

"Yup! It triggers my asthma."

"Oh! I didn't know you have asthma."

Joe chuckled. "Oh yeah! I've had it all my life."

"I hope there's no ragweed around here."

"It's hard to avoid it. One plant produces up to one billion pollen grains. They are so light they can float through the air for miles." He held her face in his hands. "Don't you worry your pretty little head about it," he said. "I get allergy shots."

"That's good." Joanne took his hand, and Joe lead the way to the pond. "This old, crooked path reminds me of my life's journey with all its twist and turns."

"You know your path wasn't really crooked. It brought you to God and to me."

"Yes, that's because God straightened it for me."

Joe pulled her into him. "I'm so glad God put you on my path. I love verses five and six of Proverbs 3. It has become my life verse."

"How's that go?"

"'Trust in the Lord with all your heart, and do not rely on your own insight. In all your ways acknowledge Him, and He will make straight your path.'"

"Imagine what our world would be like if everyone trusted God? What if everyone stopped trusting the news media. What if—"

"There would be no more fear," he said.

"Imagine all the people paralyzed by fear learning to let go and trust God." Joanne bounced up and down on her tiptoes. "Joe, this can be our mission statement: Empowering people to let go of fear and trust God."

"Perfect!"

When they reached the pond, they noticed the red canoe nestled under the weeping willow tree.

"I assumed Zack put that away for the winter when he put *Serenity* in storage."

"Well, since it's here, let's go for a ride." Joanne smiled and grabbed Joe's hand. "Come on."

Gliding across the pond, Joanne radiated with delight. She was mesmerized by the reflection of the red, yellow, and orange leaves shimmering on the clear water. "Can I paddle myself?"

"Sure." Joe passed the paddle to Joanne. "Go for it."

She paddled and paddled but she was unable to get the canoe to advance. Joe observed her struggle but didn't interfere. Soon exhaustion overcame her. She let go of the paddle, crossed her arms, and scowled at Joe. "What's wrong?"

Joe grinned. "You're going against the current. Turn around and observe the difference."

"Wow!" Joanne beamed. "This is more like it."

"See, Jo, when you go with the current, you are in the flow."

"I get it," she said. "It's like when we surrender and let God we are in the flow."

"Life is a series of changes. If we resist them, we can end up with heartache and sorrow, but if we live in a surrendered state, we will be happy."

"Here," she said, "you can have the paddle back."

"Hold on to one. Let's do tandem paddling."

"Oh! This is like dancing once you find your rhythm."

"Ya know somethin'?" Joe asked. "We make a great team."

Joanne jiggled when she giggled.

"Whoa! Don't rock the boat!"

As they paddled along together, they soaked in the healing energy of the sunshine, and enjoyed the connection with nature. Taking time from their busy schedule and lingering on the pond refreshed their bodies, minds, and souls.

"There's so much to be thankful for," Joe said. "Everywhere I look I see God's beauty."

"I agree." Gratitude swelled in Joanne's heart.

As they approached the shore, a sense of solitude engulfed

them. Joe pulled the paddles in and they enjoyed a private moment in silence, secluded from civilization.

"Ah! This is the life," Joe said, but then his smile turned into a frown. Wrinkling his brow, he fumbled in his jacket pockets. For a split second, he wondered if he had lost it.

"What's wrong, Joe?"

"Nothing!" With a sigh of relief and a gleam in his eyes, he withdrew a small, blue box and slid off the seat onto his knees. "Will you marry me, Joanne?" he asked as he slipped a big, round, brilliant-cut diamond ring on her finger.

"Yes, yes, of course!" she screamed. Stretching her arm out, she gawked at the diamond, sparkling in the sun. "It's gorgeous!" Overcome by a surge of joy, Joanne lurched forward to hug Joe. The canoe wobbled; then it tipped over, and Joe and Joanne tumbled out.

Time slowed down as they sank beneath the cold water. It seemed as if it was happening in slow motion. First, Joe surfaced, gasping for air, and then Joanne popped up, sputtering water. When she realized they were standing in water waist deep she burst out laughing. Joe took one glance at her and went into convulsions, laughing too. Clinging onto the swamped canoe, they slogged through the tall, tangled grass until they reached the edge of the water.

Joanne groaned as they pushed the canoe onto the shore. "Oh no … the Tiffany box!"

Joe held the blue box up. "I caught it floating by."

Joanne squealed. "Good catch!"

"Yes, you are," Joe said, winking at her.

REFLECTION

Both Joanne and Joe had a lot of turmoil in their lives. Did you notice how God used their problems to get their attention? They developed a strong relationship with God, and their lives were transformed. When you learn to trust God, your life will be transformed too. Do you believe God loves you?

ACTION TIP

Spend some time this week reading scripture. Sometimes when you pick up the Bible, you will read just what you need to hear.

Every day, write down one way God helped you. Talk to God. Ask Him what He wants for you. Talk to Him as a friend. He wants to have a personal relationship with you. You can sit in silence and just listen, but open your heart to hear Him.

Start your day, before you even get out of bed, with a prayer and surrender. Surrender your day to God, and see how it feels to be in the flow. Go ahead. Let go.

PETITION

Dear God,

I'm sorry for not trusting You, but it is so hard. Can you please help me to trust You?

EPILOGUE

Six months later:

hey returned from Florida at the end of February. As COVID-19 raged around the world, Joe and Joanne made the decision not to reopen Kitty's Place until the global pandemic ended. Instead, they planned to offer online courses and workshops to help people cope with the negative impacts of the coronavirus.

March 23, 2020

When her cell phone rang at six thirty in the morning, terror paralyzed Joanne. While she stood barefoot on the cold bathroom floor, warm pee rolled down her trembling legs. Finally, in a quavering voice she said, "Hello?"

Joanne's heartbeat thrashed so loud in her ears, she barely heard what the doctor said.

"Excuse me."

With cold fingers she clutched the phone and listened to the doctor fumble to find the words to say, "Joe passed away today."

Joanne dropped the phone and clapped her hands over her ears. "No!" she wailed and slumped to the floor. After her tears subsided, she picked up the phone and called Zack. "He died!" she cried. "COVID-19 killed Joe."

A crack of thunder boomed overhead. The sky opened and deposited a torrent of rain.

While they waited for Joanne to open the back door, Zack and Bambi huddled together wearing their surgical masks and listening to the pitter-patter of rain dropping down on the big, black umbrella. Zack pulled up the hood on his bright yellow rain slicker and tightened his fingers around the umbrella handle. As Bambi gripped the pot of chicken soup with both hands, she shivered and wished she could clutch her coat closer. At last, a teary Joanne opened the door.

"Oh dear," she said. "I'm so sorry. When I heard the doorbell ring, I presumed you were at the front door." Her eyebrows squished together. "I'm so confused."

"No problem," Bambi said. "I love to listen to the rhythm of the rain drops on my umbrella."

"Me too," muttered Zack. "Phut, phut, phut."

"Oh, Zack," Joanne said with a choked-up voice. "Joe loved you like a son." She swiped at her nose with a tissue. "Come here, you. I need a hug."

Zack stretched out his arms. His chin quivered. "I'm so sorry," he whispered as he held her tight.

Bambi stood in silence hugging the pot of soup. Then she let out a loud sigh. "Ya know, I'm just lost for words." Her long eyelashes grew heavy with fat tears. "I'll put the soup on the stove to heat," she said.

Joanne's eyes welled up. "Thank you so much."

Zack patted Joanne on the shoulder "I want you to know, I'm here standing by for you." He took a long inhale. "I heard the governor is issuing a statewide stay-at-home advisory today. The order prohibits social gatherings. That means Joe's funeral—"

"Joe wasn't even allowed a final farewell, and now the coronavirus will deprive him of a decent funeral!" Rubbing her palm against her chest, she slumped into Joe's chair and took a deep breath.

Zack rushed to her side and offered to get her a glass of water. She sat there staring down at her empty hands, and then Joe's words came back to her. "In your emptiness you are open to receive." She closed her eyes and prayed. "Dear God, I trust You. Please bless me with the grace to accept Your will."

Then it occurred to her, she wasn't alone in her grief. The whole world was feeling the pain of losing someone or something they loved. Maybe they had lost a loved one or a job or financial security or a familiar routine, a hug from a grandchild, the human touch. Smiles are now invisible with wearing a mask. So much loss.

When Zack handed Joanne the glass, it broke the spell. "While you were in the kitchen, I was thinking about all the loss in our world. Only a week ago, my biggest concern about the pandemic was how long would it be before I could get my eyelash extensions and nails done." Trying to compose herself she took a deep breath and sniffled. "Do you believe in the promises of sacred scripture?"

After a pause, Zack said, "I do."

"Please pass me Joe's Bible over there." She pointed to the desk. "Last week, Joe sat right here talking about the pandemic. Can you believe he's gone?" Her eyes moistened.

Zack took a deep sigh and gave her an understanding nod.

"Joe told me, 'In this crisis, there is opportunity. Opportunity for people to grow in love with God. Maybe God is using this pandemic to get people's attention, to bring people back to

Him.'" Opening the Bible to St. Paul's letter to the Romans, Joanne pushed the glasses up on her nose and squinted at the text. "These damn tears are making it all blurry," she said. "Can you read chapter eight, verse twenty-eight?"

Zack cleared his throat and read the scripture. "'We know that in all things God works for the good of those who love him, who have been called according to his purpose.'"

"That's everything, Zack: good things, bad things, this pandemic, this liminal space we are in, the trials, the joys, the sorrows. They all work for our good if we love God. He is calling us to love Him."

"I know," Zack said. "And we have been called to help people find God."

"Isn't it crazy?" Joanne smiled. "Imagine. A bunch of misfits like us—"

"Soup's ready," hollered Bambi from the kitchen.

"Mmm," Zack muttered, "it smells good." The aroma of simmering chicken soup wafted through the air.

When they entered the kitchen, a warm glow beckoned them from the cozy fireplace. Zack walked over to the window. "The rain stopped, but it's damp and raw out there." With his voice full of emotion, he said, "The fire was a great idea, Bambi."

She gave him a closed-lip smile and fidgeted with her top button.

"Yes," Joanne said. "Thank you for your thoughtfulness."

Bambi reached out and took Joanne's cold hands. "I remember when my mother died, I was freezing all the time. Grief makes you cold."

"It does." Joanne shivered and gripped Bambi's hands.

Without any warning, a dam of sorrow burst. Bambi pulled

Joanne close, and as she hugged her, she rubbed her back. "There, there."

Zack handed her a box of tissues. "Thanks," she said as she snatched a few. "You guys are the best." She blew her nose and said, "You are my family."

When Joanne settled down, they all took seats around the table and held hands as Bambi said grace.

After Joanne blew on the steaming bowl of soup, she took a sip. "Thank you, Bambi, this is delicious." She put the spoon down and sighed. "Nothing is more soul-satisfying and restorative than homemade chicken soup made with love." Joanne stared at Bambi and placed her hand on her arm. "I have an idea! How would you like to teach people how to cook with love?"

"What?"

"With the governor's stay-at-home order, people will be eating all kinds of junk and gaining weight. How about a nutrition and weight management online course, teaching people how to lose weight by accepting God's love. You know, Joe always said, 'When you love God, everything changes, including your weight.'"

"Wow! That sounds divine."

"And how about you, Zack? You can lead an online Bible study to help people cope with stress and anxiety."

"Me?" he asked. "Am I equipped for that?"

"Of course. The Holy Spirit is working in your life. He'll be helping you. Joe always said he saw something special in you."

Zack took a sharp breath. "And what about you?"

"Well, Joe and I discussed offering a free online workshop for the community. It's not easy to discern divine will. I might title the workshop, Finding God in Our Liminal Space. I'll have to pray on it." As she got to her feet she said, "But right now I need a nap."

Zack scraped one hand through his hair. "Okay, wait one minute." He disappeared and returned with a white envelope in his hand. "From Joe," he said.

Joanne staggered backward. Glancing at the sealed envelope in Zack's hand, tears rolled down her cheeks. At first, she was so bewildered, she couldn't speak. She stared at Zack. "Joe?" she asked, becoming breathless.

Zack held her. When he placed the envelope in her hand, she let out a moan and slowly turned around. In a daze, she walked into Joe's bedroom, clutching the letter next to her heart.

She hunkered down on Joe's closet floor, pulled his cotton tee shirt off a hanger, and buried her face in the soft fabric. With trembling fingers, she ripped the envelope open. In between deep inhales of Joe's scent and long sobs, she read his letter over and over and over again.

> Dear Joanne,
>
> If you are reading this letter you know it is the end of our beginning. While my life on earth is over, this ending is the beginning of my eternal life.
>
> I wrote this letter because I realized if COVID-19 got me, I'd never get a chance to say goodbye.
>
> Thank you for letting me spend the rest of my life with you. I am grateful to you for giving me the opportunity to open Kitty's Place and make a difference in people's lives. Your love made it possible for me to die a happy man. I only regret I couldn't give you the June wedding we planned.
>
> Promise me you will never forget the day we met

when you saw the word "VALUABLE" flash across your mind. Remember you are valued by God. He blessed you with the gift of bringing out the best in people. Always let your light shine. Don't let my death dim your light. Remember, I'm just a thought away.

Use this time of uncertainty to grow and to strengthen your faith to meet the needs of a post-pandemic world.

Our love story has no ending.

My love for you will never die,
Joe

Printed in the United States
by Baker & Taylor Publisher Services